FORBIDDEN PLEASURE

ERNEST MORRIS

GOOD 2 GO PUBLISHING

FORBIDDEN PLEASURE
Written by Ernest Morris
Cover Design: Davida Baldwin, Odd Ball Designs
Typesetter: Mychea
ISBN: 978-1-947340-56-5
Copyright © 2020 Good2Go Publishing
Published 2020 by Good2Go Publishing
7311 W. Glass Lane • Laveen, AZ 85339
www.good2gopublishing.com
https://twitter.com/good2gobooks
G2G@good2gopublishing.com
www.facebook.com/good2gopublishing
www.instagram.com/good2gopublishing

ACKNOWLEDGEMENTS

First and foremost let me begin by sending out my condolences to everyone that has lost a loved one because of this COVID-19 epidemic. We will rise up and conquer this because we're stronger.

Secondly, I would like to thank the man above for helping me understand how valuable talent is and that it shouldn't be wasted. It took me a while, but I now understand my worth. Every day I try to make a difference in this world, and as hard as it is to make a breakthrough, I finally feel like it's about to pay off. If I can show one person how important life is, then I have done my job.

I would like to thank everyone at GOOD2GO PUBLISHING for continuing to see the best in me. Even when I was at a low point in my life, you continued to trust me. It's because of you that I can walk around with my head held high and be proud of my success.

My goal is to be constructive, and not destructtive. There are many obstacles that we will face in our time on earth, but never back down, and most importantly, never give up. The only thing worse than being blind is having sight with no vision.

I would like to give a shout out to a bunch of people. If I missed anyone, it was not on purpose. Those people are: Ashley, Sherry, Amy, Ms. T, Samantha, Demina, Le'Shea, Sahmeer, Shayana, Stud, Mello, Yah, Banger, Reek, Dread, Swag, Yola, Mack, Mike, Rich, Jay, Bruce, Kelly, Stacy, Heather, Kelsey, Anaya, Aliyah, Cyn, Candy, Cassandra, Liz, Zu Zu, Kayley, Monique, Leneek, Dwunna, Kimmy, Melissa, Nasira, Quill, Rasheed, Walid, Chubb, Maurice, Theresa, Loveanna, Tamara, Ed, and Shamika.

Finally, I want to thank you, the readers. Without you, we authors wouldn't have a career. You make it possible for us to continue expressing our visions through writing. Please continue to support our brand and purchase my new novel BREAKING THE CHAINS, on Amazon.com.

ONE

"Mmmmmm, baby, that feels really good."

Taylor's body was on fire as her lover devoured her insides. She felt like she was going to release her juices at any moment. With her back arched in the air and her legs spread wide, she began rotating her hips in a circular motion. She could feel her explosion getting closer and closer. The heat radiated off of her pussy like the fire from a fireplace. Her body went into convulsions. She continued shaking uncontrollably as the liquids from her pussy poured from her body like a faucet.

"Damn, baby, I can't stop this orgasm," Taylor moaned with her eyes shut tightly, squeezing her pussy muscles together around her lover's tongue. "What are you doing to me?"

"Exactly what you wanted me to do. This is what you wanted, right?"

"Yeesssss, now stop talking and finish giving

me what I need," Taylor replied, her eyes rolling into the back of her head.

No more words were spoken as she continued to be dominated. Her lover's tongue was doing things that she never imagined being done before. It went from her clitoris to the crack of her ass, then back deep inside her swollen walls. Just when she thought that it couldn't get any better, she felt something cold being rubbed across her belly button, down toward her vagina. That's when she realized that it was an ice cube. At the same time, Taylor felt her anal area being violated by two fingers. Excitement took over her inhibitions. The ice melted within seconds. Then there was a light breeze, which Taylor realized was her lover blowing into her pussy. It sent her into another trembling orgasm.

"Oh my God, baby, I need you inside me," Taylor mumbled as she came down from another explosion.

She reached out for her lover's penis and felt something different. Her eyes popped open, and what she saw took her breath away. It was her next-door neighbor.

"What are you doing?"

"Shhhh, just let me please you. I know I'm better than he is," her neighbor whispered, trying to go back to work on Taylor's body.

As hard as she tried to resist temptation mentally, her body physically wasn't having it. Taylor suddenly gave in to the warm tongue that felt miraculously better than anything her husband had ever done. It flicked and twirled, fast, then slow, in and out of her hole like a snake. Every thirty seconds it would pay extra attention to her extra sensitive clit that had swelled up. She allowed those same fingers that previously entered her butthole, to penetrate her walls again. As her pussy was being pleased by a tongue, her ass was being pleased by a pair of fingers.

No longer unable to contain her excitement, Taylor's climax started building up. She was on the verge of another earth-quaking explosion. Her nipples were hard as rocks. She began pinching and squeezing them together before placing one into her mouth.

"Mmmmmm!" Her moans became louder and louder. "Ahhhhh, oh my God. Yeesssss."

Unexpectedly, before she could get off, Taylor woke up from her dream. She was soaking wet. When she looked over to the right side of the bed, her husband was still sound asleep. The dream felt so real that she got up to check the rest of her bedroom for any signs of her neighbor. Coming to the conclusion that no one else was there, she went into the bathroom to clean up.

That dream seemed all too real for her. She removed her panties and stuck a finger inside her pussy. It was drenched, only confirming that she did have some type of orgasm in her sleep. Taylor washed up and came out of the bathroom. She placed her soaked nightgown in the hamper and threw on another. As she made her way back over toward the bed, she noticed her neighbor's bedroom light on. Their shades were ajar just enough to see inside. Curiosity caused her to take a peek. They were standing near the window naked.

"Oh my," Taylor mumbled in awe at the sight of her neighbors.

What really caught her attention was the person standing in the background of the room. She had seen her before. It was their coworker. Taylor had seen her over there a few times a week. Never did she think that this would be one of the reasons. She continued to watch them for a few minutes as they engaged in all kinds of foreplay without a care in the world about who saw them.

Taylor could feel herself getting turned on again. Her hand started making its way down to her pussy. She never put any panties back on, which gave her the access she needed to her tunnel of love. Never taking her eyes off the threesome that was taking place across the lawn, she placed one leg on the window ledge and stuck one, then two fingers inside and started flicking her clit. It felt so good.

Suddenly, Taylor heard her husband move. She quickly adjusted the blinds on the window and rushed back over to her side of the bed, easing under the covers next to him. He turned over, placing his arm around her so they were in a spooning position. She pretended she was asleep, but the scene of her neighbors and the dream she had made her horny as hell.

Taylor reached behind her, rubbing her husband's dick, trying to wake him up. He yawned, then grabbed her breast and squeezed.

"Hey you!" He began kissing the back of her neck. "What a feeling to wake up to."

He quickly removed her nightgown, then his clothes. He tried to make love to her, but she didn't want to make love this time. Taylor just wanted to be fucked, and that's exactly what they did. The whole time her mind was on the neighbors.

~ ~ ~

"Morning,"

"Good morning to you," Steve replied, giving

Taylor a kiss on the cheek. He poured himself a cup of coffee and sat down at the kitchen table. "What got into you last night?"

"What do you mean?" Taylor giggled.

"You know exactly what I'm talking about, Mrs. Smith."

"What, I can't get a little freaky for my handsome husband who will be leaving us again today for who knows how long this time?" Taylor said, wrapping her arms around his neck. He pulled her into his lap and started kissing her neck.

"You know everything I do is for you and our baby girl, right?" Steve squeezed her ass, causing Taylor to let out a soft moan.

"Yuck, that's nasty. Get a room, you two," their ten-year-old daughter said, standing in the doorway giggling at her parents.

"Come here, you little munchkin," Steve said, reaching for his daughter.

Trinity ran into his awaiting arms. She was their only child, and they treated her like a princess. Whenever Steve was home, he would shower her with all the love in the world. The souvenirs he brought back from overseas helped also. Each night before bed they would FaceTime each other. That was one of the many promises that he tried to keep. No matter what he was doing, he made time to say good night. Trinity was the spitting image of her mother. She had all of her features.

Steve Smith was the Lt. Commander on the USS *Darling*, and had already been stationed out to sea for the last year. He had come home for a brief leave to surprise his family, but now he was about to be deployed again. Even though it would be hard to cope with, they knew that he had a job to do. It didn't make his absence from his family any easier, but he knew they would be okay.

"I need to go take a quick shower before we head out to the airport," Steve said, giving his daughter and wife a kiss.

An hour later, Taylor and her family were pulling up to AVP International Airport out in

Wilkes-Barre, Pennsylvania. At nine o'clock in the morning, the lines were beginning to form with passengers, ready to head out.

"I will call you once we're up in the air," Steve said, giving his wife and daughter a kiss.

"Bye, Daddy."

"It's not goodbye, sweetheart, it's see you later," Steve reminded her. To him, goodbye meant you'd never see someone again, and he planned on coming back home to his family. "I love you."

Once he walked through the airport doors, Taylor pulled out into traffic, heading back home. As she drove down the highway toward Scranton, her mind went back to what she saw her neighbors doing. They didn't seem like the kinky type, but you never know who you're living next to or what kind of behavior they will display behind closed doors. That is what intrigued her. She took them for the stuck-up type. Boy, was she wrong about that.

Later that night, Taylor received the call that

would change her life forever. She found out that her husband, soulmate, high school sweetheart, and father of her child had been living a double life. He had a whole other family in Philadelphia. While he was away, Steve had slept with a couple of women and had gotten one of them pregnant. Instead of him coming clean with it, he kept it a secret and had been taking care of them both for the last year.

The woman had found a number in his phone and written it down. With confirmation that Steve was on a plane heading back to his ship, the girl called the number and spilled the beans to Taylor. She was livid to hear about this other family.

While he was away, Taylor started planning to file for a divorce. Steve came clean and said that it was a one-time thing and that he made a mistake. He manipulated her into staying together for the sake of their daughter, and Taylor stayed because she believed him. This would be the beginning of the end.

TWO

"This is control to all areas. Commence your 11:15 sitting count, commence your 11:15 sitting count," the officer announced over the PA system.

"Count time. Everyone sit up and remain seated until the other officer does his cross count. No talking," Officer Jankoski yelled out as she began her midday count.

This was her normal routine every day at the prison she worked in. When she yelled, the inmates would sit up on their bunks and wait to be counted. Everyone knew that she was crazy, but there would always be one that would try his hand. She walked over to his bunk and kicked it twice.

"Sit up for count. I'm not going to tell you again."

"You don't have to kick my bed," Lyons snapped, hopping up from his pillow. The agitation in his voice was apparent. "You dumb bitch."

Officer Jankoski finished her count then called over the radio for the area 4 sergeant. Everyone on the block was up now, waiting to see how this would play out. They knew it wasn't going to end well for the inmate. Once count was over, a team of officers came to escort Lyons to the hole.

This is how it worked in prison. You got smart or talked back to a staff member, you bought yourself a one-way ticket to isolation. Officer Jankoski was pulled from the block so she could do her write-up. She decided to do it on the computer that was located in the medical department.

Officer Karen Jankoski was thirty-nine years old. She had been working in the Department of Corrections for over six years now and had a long way to go. She was a college grad and a reserve in the military, which meant that she was very capable of handling herself in any situation. She was a single, attractive white female, with no kids. The reason for that was she just didn't have time.

Her life was complicated.

"Who did you send to the bucket now?" a voice asked from behind her.

Karen looked up from the monitor into the hazel eyes of Carla. "Some inmate that was acting like an asshole at count time. All he had to do was keep his mouth shut and wait until I did my count. Then he could have laid back down and went to sleep. He had to keep talking out the side of his neck though."

"So he got what he deserved then?" Carla asked.

"Yep! I guess he did," Karen replied with a smile. She could feel Carla's hot breath on the back of her neck, making her hairs stick up. She slowly shifted in her seat.

"What's wrong with you?" Carla giggled, noticing the way she was fidgeting around. She slowly slid her hand over Karen's shoulder, down the right side of her blouse until she reached her breast. "Are you okay?"

By this time, Karen had stopped typing and

closed her eyes. Her breathing got deeper as her heart sped up from Carla fondling her breast. It was a gentle touch that made her pussy moist. Carla's hand suddenly moved down her stomach, toward the waistline of her black uniform pants. In order for her hand to get inside, Carla would have to unbuckle her utility belt, and Karen knew this; that's why she stopped her.

"Not here. We don't know who will walk past and see us. Let's go down to y'all's break room. No one will be in there for a while, right?" Karen asked, getting up from her seat.

Without answering, Carla walked out of the room first and headed down the hall. As she walked past one of the inmate porters, she gave him a nod and smile that said so much more than words could say. He must have picked up on it, because he smiled back, shaking his head. Karen followed Carla into the break room. Soon as they walked out of eyesight of the door, Karen was all over her.

She stuck a hand down the waistband of

Carla's scrubs and slid a finger across her pussy lips. That sent chills up and down Carla's spine. She stuck her tongue out, inviting Carla to reciprocate. She gladly accepted the invite with her own.

"Oh my God," Carla moaned each time Karen fingered her. Her arms were wrapped around her neck tightly as she leaned against the table.

They thought the heat was coming from their bodies, but it was really hot in the room. Karen walked over and opened up a window. By the time she walked back around the table, Carla had her scrubs down to her ankles and was lying on top of the table, exposing her cleanly shaved pussy. It was glistening from her juices that flowed out freely.

"Hurry up and make me cum, and I'll hook you up when we get off," Carla purred, sticking a finger inside her hole. Each time she pulled it out and stuck it back in, it made a squooshing sound.

Karen kneeled down between her legs and stuck her tongue deep inside, twirling it over her clit. Carla arched her ass up in the air to give her better access to her tunnel of love. Placing her legs over her shoulder, Karen began devouring her insides at a rapid pace. Carla's pussy smelled like strawberries from the perfume she sprayed on earlier. It had Karen's senses at an all-time high.

"Ohhh shiiiittt, I'm about to cum," Carla moaned, grabbing Karen's hair and pulling her face deeper inside her pussy.

Ten seconds later, Carla was squirting all over her face. Karen stood up pulling Carla off the table, giving her a passionate kiss, letting her taste her own juices. Carla grabbed a couple of napkins off the table, then wiped herself with them. She pulled up her scrubs and tied them.

"I'll swing past your house after work and we can finish this."

"That's if they don't mandate me," Karen replied, checking her uniform to make sure everything was intact before they left the break room.

As they were walking out the door, two nurses

were walking toward them with food. They spoke to officer Jankoski then headed inside. Relieved that they didn't suspect anything, both women went their separate ways. Karen couldn't wait until she got off of work.

"I knew they were in there doing something," one of the nurses whispered as they walked out of the break room.

"It smelled like coochie up in there."

Both women laughed as they headed back to their respective stations. The inmate porters were sitting at the table playing cards and watching the female nurses strutting around flirtatiously with their tight-fitting, see-through scrubs on. Some of them liked the little attention they got from the inmates, as well as the other staff members. As long as they looked but didn't touch, everything was all good.

Carla Campanella was one of those nurses. She had been working in the Department of Corrections as a nurse's assistant for a year before she graduated and became an RN. Now she was making a name for herself, and it wasn't a good one. It was the one you would never want in the workplace. She was known to most as the prison slut. The one who never had a problem giving the next man, or woman, what they wanted.

When she first started, all the COs tried to get in her pants, but she played hard to get. Once she finally gave in to one, it was over. He told everyone else how easy it would be, and they all took turns having their way with her. Even some inmates thought that they could, but never tried, knowing what the consequences would be. Instead, they enjoyed hearing the stories of the ones who did. Her and Officer Jankoski got close as time went by because of their association with a counselor that worked there. They would all sit and chat about everything.

One day they all went out for drinks at a pub in Carbondale. By the end of the night they were in a hotel room having a threesome. That was when Carla realized that she was bisexual. There were two forms of lesbians, fem and butch. Karen was considered butch because she was more of a man in the relationship. She was always the one laying the pipe, not the one receiving it. Everything was good until feelings started to get involved.

THREE

"*I processed your paperwork to get you out* of here. I'm just waiting to hear back from Central Office," Tara said, sitting at her desk. She was talking to an inmate about getting him out of prison early. "I'm asking you to be patient, and I'll let you know as soon as I hear something."

Dread stood up and headed toward the door. He had been trying to get out of prison for over six months with no success thus far. Before he walked out, he turned back to Tara. "Thank you so much for your help."

"No problem, sir. I'm going to fax those papers over now."

Tara Carmola was a guidance counselor in the prison. She had over seven years' experience in psychology and criminal behavior. She was hired as a correctional officer, but realized that her knowledge was needed elsewhere and crossed over. Now she was taking on an overwhelming caseload of 160 inmates, and it was far from easy. As much as she wanted to complain, she knew that she was the voice that they needed.

Tara did everything she could not to be one of those staff members that liked to spin others. If she couldn't do something right then and there, she would just come straight out and say so. She was one of those people that was straightforward about everything, which made everyone respect her more than anyone else.

"Are we going out this weekend?" Karen asked, sticking her head in the door.

Tara smiled at her friend. "I have nothing else going on," she replied.

"Good, me, you and Carla then. I talked to her earlier, and she's down for whatever."

Karen and Carla really didn't do much talking. They were too busy doing other things, but she knew that she would go out with them. If not, she would convince her later on tonight when they were together. She had a way of getting what she wanted.

"Okay, well I have a lot of work to do, so I'll call you later."

"Damn, you kicking me out already. I can take a hint," Karen joked as she left Tara's office so she could finish her work.

~ ~ ~

Stone Wildes spotted the Philadelphia International Airport ten miles out. "Control Center, November One, Two, Three, Tango Foxtrot has the airport in sight."

"N123TF, contact the tower on 2180. Good day to you."

"Good day." He turned to the channel. "Control tower, N123TF 9 miles to the north at ten thousand. Request straight in for runway two zero."

"N123TF, I have you in sight. Cleared for the visual to two zero."

"Tango Fox, cleared for the visual." Stone lined up on the runway, reduced power, put in his first notch of flaps, and dialed in eight thousand feet. The autopilot began the descent. Five miles out, he dropped the landing gear, slowing the airplane further, then put in 35 degrees of flaps and let the airplane slow to approach speed.

At the sound of the gear lowering, Stone's two passengers turned and looked out the window. At about five hundred feet above ground level, he slowed to reference speed of 107 knots, crossed the runway threshold, and settled smoothly onto the tarmac. As he put in the final notch of flaps to dump lift and began to brake, he spotted an Aston Martin parked on the ramp outside, and a tall blond woman wearing slacks leaning against it.

Stone turned off the runway, stopped, and ran his after-landing checklist, then called the tower and was cleared to taxi to the ramp. A man waved him in next to the Aston Martin, then chocked the nosewheel. Stone pulled the throttles back to the shutoff position and waited for the engines to spool down before turning off the main switch, which shut down the instrument panel. He struggled out of his seat, opened the cabin door, grabbed his backpack, kicked down the folding stairs, and let the passengers out of the plane first.

Gina Wildes met them at the bottom of the steps, planted an enthusiastic kiss on the first man's lips, then gave Stone and the other passenger a hug.

"Welcome back, baby," she said. "We've got dinner at seven at the restaurant." Gina wrapped her arm around the man's arm as they walked toward the car.

Stone retrieved the couple of bags from the forward luggage compartment and tossed them into the trunk of the Aston Martin along with the other bags, which used nearly all of the available luggage space, then got into the passenger seat, letting Gina and her man get in the back. The other passenger hopped in the driver's seat.

"I'm ready for a drink or two," the man said. "Then I'll be ready for something else." He stuck a hand between her legs and squeezed her pussy through her slacks.

"Stop it. There are other people in the car. You'll have to wait until we're alone."

"I'll try, but I may get the shakes from not seeing you. Just thinking about you always makes me horny," he said, whispering in her ear.

"Awwww, Steve, you say the sweetest things," Gina said, giving him another kiss.

After being dropped off at the airport in Wilkes-Barre, Steve walked over to the private plane that was waiting for him and headed to Philly to see his other family. The pilot was Gina's brother, and the other passenger was her sister-in-law. Gina and Stone had inherited a lot of money after their wealthy parents had been killed in a boat bombing over in Iraq. Steve was the one who had led the recovery. They became close over the next year, and feelings got involved, causing them to fall in love. Gina became pregnant and had a little boy.

At first Stone thought Steve was just trying to get their money, but after getting to know him, he realized that he really did love his sister. As long as she was happy, so was he.

Nancy started the engine, which emitted a

pleasing, guttural noise, then waited for the gate to open so they could leave.

"Good flight?" Gina asked, holding his hand.

"Boring flight—the best kind. I read the newspaper and did the crossword."

"Your eyes say that you wanted to be doing something nasty."

Steve smirked, then guided her hand over the crouch of his pants. "You sure we have to wait until later? He is getting real impatient."

Gina instantly became moist at the feeling of his rock-hard dick. She couldn't wait to get home so they could have a quickie before they went out to dinner. Forty minutes later they pulled into the driveway of their house just on the outskirts of Philly. Steve helped Stone grab the luggage and followed the ladies into the house.

Steve and Gina headed up to the master suite. He dumped the contents of his bags on the bed and threw all the dirty clothes in the hamper in the closet. By the time he had finished putting his clothes in the drawer, Gina was lying on the bed naked, awaiting his touch that she had been craving since exiting the airport. Steve got on the bed, spreading her legs, then dove headfirst into her pussy.

"Oh shit," Gina moaned, trying to move away from his tongue, but he held tight.

"Don't move," he said as she was gasping from how good his tongue felt.

She tried, but couldn't help herself because it was feeling too good to her. She was grinding her pussy on his face and watching him grin as he performed his sexual act. Steve shifted his body so he was now on top, and entered her, stroking at a rapid pace. Gina took everything he had to offer.

Steve had her legs pinned behind her head as he brought his body up and down on her pelvis. In a matter of minutes, the two of them were both cumming in unison.

"So I guess we should get ready for dinner now."

"Yes, I guess you're right. Let me take a quick shower," Gina replied, heading toward the bathroom. She turned around and faced Steve, who was still lying on the bed catching his breath. "Care to join me?"

"Why yes I do," Steve answered.

He leaped off the bed and followed her into the bathroom. Gina turned the shower head on, and immediately the windows and mirror fogged up. The quick shower that they were supposed to take turned into an hour of sexual activities. Even though they were drained, they still kept their dinner appointment.

~ ~ ~

The restaurant on City Line Avenue was packed. Luckily they had reservations. Once they were seated by the sexy hostess, another very pretty waitress came over to take their orders. Gina and Steve ordered drinks and appetizers to start off with. The waitress headed over to the bar to make their drinks, while Gina removed her jacket to get a bit more comfortable.

"So how does Stone feel about losing his partner?"

"He's not losing him. Ben will still help with the writing, at least until he finds someone else to take his place," Gina said. "This is all for the best."

"He'll be one busy S-O-B."

"He seems to like it that way. Stone says Ben always got bored while they were waiting for different people to get back to them. That won't be a problem anymore. By the way, how is the divorce coming along? You told me that you were leaving her, but you're still living there when you're not with me."

"Baby, these things take time," Steve said, leaning in and grabbing her hand. "I do have a daughter with her, which doesn't make this any easier. I'm just trying to find a reason to make it happen quicker."

"Our son needs you too, Steve," Gina complained. "What about him? He needs a father figure in his life to be around him and teach him manly things. My brother has been more of a father than you have. I understand that your daughter needs you, but she doesn't. From what you said, y'all not even having sex anymore, right?"

"No, we're not," he lied, thinking about the sex they had last night.

"So what do you need me to do?" All Gina wanted was Steve all to herself. She would give anything to have that one thing.

"Just be patient, baby. That's all I'm asking."

"I am. I just want to wake up to you all the time."

Steve stood up and sat beside her. They were in a nice quiet booth in the back of the restaurant where no one could really see what they were doing. He stuck his hand between her legs, moving her panties to the side, and stuck a finger deep inside her pussy. Gina closed her eyes and bit down on her bottom lip. She opened her legs wider, causing her dress to lift even higher, exposing her clean-shaved pussy lips, for better access.

"Don't worry, you will have everything you want real soon," Steve whispered in her ear as he continued to finger her like they were the only two people there.

Unbeknownst to them, someone was watching them. They had been snapping pictures of the couple since they sat down. Once the waitress came back with their food, the person that had been taking pictures got up and left.

"Time to upload these pics on the internet," the photographer mumbled, heading out the door.

FOUR

Taylor finished her shopping at Macy's, then headed over to the T-Mobile store that was on the ground floor of the Steamtown Mall. She wanted to buy a new cell phone for her daughter. She also thought about buying her cheating-ass husband something, but that thought quickly evaporated from her mind. What she had found out about him still left a sour taste in her mouth0. A01ll this time, there was no telling how many times he had probably cheated on her. She had her own little secret also.

Taylor looked around at all the different phones and found a couple that she thought her daughter would like. Not able to choose between the final two, she bought them both, deciding to keep whichever one Trinity didn't like, for herself. She was waiting for the cashier to run her credit card and place the phones and accessories in a bag, when she looked up and saw an old friend walking through the door. She froze and tried to keep her face expressionless.

"Well hello there," Boris said, striding toward her. He had this smile on his face that spoke a thousand words.

She held up an arm to fend him off. "Please," she said.

Actually, Boris was more than just an old friend. He was a fling that she had one night when she went to an after-hours club with her neighbor. She was drunk and horny, and he was there. Nothing ever came of it, and even though he knew that it was only a one-time thing, he still used to try for more whenever he saw her.

"Please, what? Aren't you glad to see me?"

"I am not."

"I'm sorry I that I keep bothering you, but I really do like you, Taylor, and I'm hoping that we can at least be friends," he said. "I might be a real nuisance to you, but deep down inside I know you're loving the attention."

As much as she wanted to deny it, she was

kind of enjoying the fact that she could still have a man chasing after her.

"We can't do this, Boris," she began. "I have a family at home, and you're trying to ruin it."

"Were you thinking about your family when I had your legs in the air, eating your pussy? Or maybe you were thinking about them when I had you ass up, face down, dicking you from behind while you were screaming out in pleasure?" Boris moved closer to Taylor, whispering in her ear. "From the looks of it, you're looking flustered right now. Are you wondering what it would feel like if I was to take you right here, right now?"

"I think you need to back up. Ain't nobody thinking about you."

Taylor had *liar* written all over her face. Something about his presence made her want to drop her pants wherever, whenever for him. Just his smile alone could have any woman's panties soaking wet. She grabbed her card and the bag with the new phones, then started for the door. Boris followed her out. Taylor took the escalator down to the basement where she had parked. When she reached her car and turned around, he was right on her heels.

"Can you please stop following me?"

"Is that what you really want?" he asked, getting so close, that she could smell the mint Tic-Tac he had in his mouth. "I'm sensing something different." Their lips touched.

Boris reached around her waist and squeezed her ass. Taylor felt like a little kid in a candy store. Her body melted in his arms as she gave in to his suaveness. With his other hand, he reached down and unbuttoned her pants, then stuck it inside, running a finger over her pussy lips.

"Ssssssss," Taylor hissed, looking around to see if anyone was paying them any attention. Because of where she had parked, it was out of direct eyesight of anyone who was entering or leaving the mall. "Damn, that feels good."

Knowing that he had her where he wanted her, Boris removed his hand from her pants. Taylor gave him a blank stare as he walked away.

"So you're just gonna leave me like this?"

"Yup," was all he said as he walked back into the mall.

Taylor couldn't believe how he just dismissed her after she was finally going to give him another taste. She got into her car and drove home.

~ ~ ~

Later that night Taylor lay in bed restless. Trinity was asleep in her room, and of course her husband wasn't there. She had been noticing a sudden change in his behavior. Recently he hadn't been calling every night to FaceTime with his daughter, and when she did talk to him, it was only a brief conversation. Even though she knew about his other family, she was still in denial. She just wanted the best for her daughter.

As she lay there watching that new show on USA called *Dare Me*, she heard her neighbor's car pulling into the driveway. Taylor peeked out the window just in time to see Ashley exiting her SUV. She looked up and waved hi. Taylor waved back, realizing that she had been caught peeping.

Ashley headed inside the house momentarily, then came back out, heading over to Taylor's house. She knocked on the door and waited for her to answer.

"Hey," Taylor said, opening the door.

"Hey, T. I just wanted to know if you had any plans this weekend?"

"No, not that I know of. Why?"

"Me and a couple of my friends are going to go out to have some drinks, and I was wondering if you would like to join us? It's nothing crazy. Just a couple of friends from work, enjoying some downtime, that's all."

"I'll have to let you know because my husband went back to his ship, and I have no one here to watch my daughter," Taylor said.

"If you like, I can have my daughter sit over here with her, or they can stay at my house while we're out. I'm sure it won't be a problem."

Taylor thought about it for a minute. It had been a lil minute since she actually went out. The last time she went out, she ended up in bed with another man.

"You don't have to give me an answer now. Take your time and let me know before this weekend so I can let my friends know that we have a plus one."

"Okay, I'll do that."

"Have a good night, girl." Ashley smiled.

"Good night!" Taylor replied, closing the door.

Taylor went upstairs, checked on her daughter, who was still sound asleep, and then went back to her bedroom to get some rest. As she lay on her bed, she thought about what she would wear if she decided to tag along with her neighbor and her friends. Her mind began to drift back to that night when she was peeping at them having a sexcapade through the window. Were they trying to lure her into their circle so they could get in her panties? Just the thought of that happening had her pussy moistening up.

"Damn, I'm a freak," she mumbled to herself.

She reached over to her nightstand, dug through her panty drawer, and pulled out one of the many sex toys she kept hidden inside. It was her favorite vibrating silver bullet. It was nine inches long and thicker than a pickle. It had a cord attached so she could either plug it in or simply use the batteries that were inside it.

Taylor turned it on to see how strong the batteries were. The loud buzzing noise confirmed that they were still practically brand new. She removed her pajama pants and leaned back on her pillows, positioning herself comfortably on the bed. With one hand she slid her Victoria's Secret panties to the side. Then with the one that was holding the vibrator, she slowly rubbed it across her clitoris, sending a tingling sensation throughout her body.

"Mmmmmm," she moaned, rotating her hips.

Inch by inch, Taylor slid the bullet inside her pussy. It felt so good when it hit her G-spot, bringing her to her first orgasm. She gave herself two more before retiring for the night.

"What are you doing to me?" Taylor asked, shaking her head as if someone was with here.

FIVE

In bed after dinner, Ashley threw a leg over Karen's and stuck her tongue in her ear. Karen responded by squeezing one of her breasts.

"Now that I have your attention." She smirked, sucking on her ear momentarily.

"You have it. Now what?"

"I wanted to bring up a subject that I have not broached since our last encounter."

"Why haven't you broached it, then?" Karen replied, using the same word that she just used.

Karen and Ashley had been seeing each other off and on for over two years before deciding to move in together. That was the deal-breaker for their relationship, and they embraced it. Ashley also had worked at the prison, but left to go back to work at the hospital. The pay was better, and she got to treat the patients like human beings. At the prison, it seemed that no matter what, you were always treated like a criminal. Most of the guards didn't care what you were there for, or that people could change. In their eyes, once a criminal, always a criminal.

Ashley couldn't subject herself to that kind of bigotry any longer. That was the reason she had to move on with her career. Karen stayed at the prison because she was making a lot of money. Even though she told herself that she would never become a sergeant, the thought always crossed her mind, especially now.

"Because the last occasion got a little bit crazy."

"Which occasion are we talking about?" Karen asked, already knowing the answer. She just wanted to hear Ashley say it.

"You know exactly what I'm talking about. Anyway, I'm thinking another potential threesome. This time, maybe we can bring in our neighbor from next door. Her husband is always gone, and I can tell that she is missing some excitement in her life," Ashley stated. "Baby, I seen it in her eyes that she is curious. You seen the way she was watching us the last time we did it."

"Yeah, but we just can't assume that she would be with it. We have to be certain first."

"I suppose so," Ashley said. She hadn't thought about that when she asked her to go out with them. How could she tell Taylor that they were going out to a gay bar, then afterward, going back to the crib for an all-out orgy? "I'll take her out to lunch tomorrow and see if I can get a feel for her."

"Maybe I should do it. She only knows you because of me," Karen said.

"Trust me, I got this," Ashley winked.

Karen smiled because she knew what she was thinking. She wished that she could see it, but she had to work. She gave Ashley a kiss and then turned the night lamp off so she could get some rest. Ashley watched TV for a while, and then she also fell asleep.

~ ~ ~

The infirmary was packed to capacity because of inmates catching the flu. They even had people sleeping in the dayroom. The next person that got it, they would have to lock down that particular block because there wasn't any more room to place them in medical. Everyone hoped that it didn't come to that point.

Nurses, doctors, and other staff members were working overtime to figure out a solution to the problem. The infirmary officers were getting frustrated because the count kept changing, and they had to keep moving people from bed to bed.

It had gotten so bad that they transferred a couple of patients to another institution temporarily, fearing that they might get exposed to the virus. The inmate porters were constantly cleaning with bleach and wearing protective masks so that they wouldn't become ill and take it back to the blocks with them. Certain precautions were in place in the event that a staff member brought it into the facility.

Carla had just arrived for work. She thought that she was going to be in the pharmacy, but was switched at the last minute for another nurse.

"Carla, you will be working in the pharmacy

today," the RN supervisor said as they stood outside of the nurse's station conversing. "We're gonna have Kayley here, and, Amanda, you will be helping her."

Kayley was a trauma nurse that was employed through a temp agency. She didn't have the same job security as the other nurses, which meant that anything she did wrong, her contract could be immediately canceled. However, she was really good at her job and was seeking a long-term contract with the option to hire full-time. She just had to make it through the probationary stages.

Amanda was a nurse's assistant, probably the best assistant you could ever ask for. She did all of the dirty jobs, never complaining about it. She was a full-time worker with weekends and holidays off. Everyone there loved her because she cared about the patients despite what they were there for. She was the type that never brought problems from home to work and never took her work home with her. She did her job and did it well.

"Did my station change also?" Keri asked, thinking that she was switching too.

"No! Everyone else is at their same spot. Let's take this flu seriously, and please protect yourselves so you don't take anything back home with you to your families."

Once their quick meeting was over, everyone went to their respective stations to begin their shift. Carla and Sara were in the pharmacy, getting the supplies and prescriptions ready. They would be handing out the midday meds in about an hour. Sara would be going down to take the RHU inmates their meds, while Carla would go help Kayley with the insulin line.

Amanda grabbed the nebulizer machine so she could go do her vital checks. She headed down the hall to the isolation rooms, where two of the inmates had it worse than the others.

"Good afternoon, Mr. Johnson," she said, entering Iso 1. "Just have to check your vitals to make sure you're okay."

"How are you doing, Ms. A?"

"I'm good. Just trying not to get this flu that's running around here," Amanda replied.

She took his vitals and moved on to the next room. By the time she finished attending to all of the patients, it was time to call the insulin line. Kayley told the officer that she was ready, and he called control. That went quickly also.

After Amanda filled all the patients' water jugs and changed her patient that was suffering from dementia, she went back into the office with the rest of the staff. The other two nurses left to take care of some other things, and Kayley and Amanda sat in the office talking.

"Did you hear about Thomas going to the hole for taking unprescribed medicine?"

"Yeah, I heard about that when I came to work. One of the workers was talking about it with the officer, and they said he refused his urine."

"That alone makes him guilty, even if he didn't do anything."

"Oh well, he brought that on himself for being stupid enough to use the stuff," Kayley said as if she was mad at him but was relieved that he was gone.

Kayley had been having problems with him since she first started, and it trickled all the way up to the management department. He kept trying to tell her how to do her job, even telling her supervisor about it. That caused friction in the workplace. She put on a fake smile just to get by because she was only a temp. All the while, she was waiting for him to do anything that she could use to get him out of there. Luckily she didn't have to do anything because he had already sealed his own fate.

"Hey, girls," Officer Jankoski said, walking up to the window, interrupting their conversation.

"What's up?" they both replied in unison.

"Where do they have Carla working at today?"

"Oh, she's in the pharmacy," Amanda replied.

She thanked them, then headed down the hall toward the pharmacy. The infirmary officer was sitting in the side room on the computer, looking at pictures.

"What are you up to?"

"Looking for some new workers. I lost two, so I have to hire two," the officer said, finishing up what he was doing.

Karen and the officer talked a few more minutes before she knocked on the window to the pharmacy. When Carla opened the gate, she smiled at her friend.

"What's up?"

Karen made sure no one else was inside with her before she spoke. "Just checking to make sure you didn't forget about this weekend."

"How the hell can I? Shit, that's all I've been thinking about," she replied. "Do you know where we're going this time?"

"Probably the same place. However, we may or may not have a newcomer. I'm waiting on confirmation now from Ashley." Before Carla could respond, her supervisor and the lieutenant came walking through the door. "I'll keep you posted on that later."

"Okay," Carla said, closing the gate back.

Karen headed back over to her block because her break was now over. She wondered how the conversation with Taylor was going.

SIX

"Thank you for inviting me out to lunch," Taylor said. They were enjoying a nice meal at a small cafe on Lackawanna Avenue. "I needed this after all I've been going through the last couple of weeks."

"Care to talk about it?"

"I'd rather not at this moment. It has nothing to do with you, so don't think that. I'm just not comfortable sharing something so bad right now."

"You're not sick or nothing right? I mean you're not walking around here with that hot shit with your freaky ass?" Ashley joked. Taylor laughed and shook her head no. "Oh, 'cause I was about to say."

This was the first time the two of them had ever been alone with each other, but they were having a good time. They talked for like forty-five minutes before the waitress came back with their check and placed it on the table. Both women reached for it at the same time. A bolt of electricity shot through their bodies, causing both of them to jump back. They laughed again.

"I got this," Ashley said, reaching into her purse for her wallet.

"No, let me. It's the least I can do," Taylor blurted out. "You have done enough by inviting me out."

"Okay, if you insist."

Taylor reached inside her purse and retrieved her credit card. As she went to stick it into the check holder, Ashley grabbed it, causing their fingers to touch, sending another strange wave through their bodies. She snatched it out of her hand and placed some cash in it. Taylor's body was on fire, but she still didn't understand why. The two of them talked for another thirty minutes before leaving the cafe.

The whole time Ashley talked, Taylor couldn't think about anything other than getting back home to her thick black dildo. Her pussy was itching for some attention. Maybe it had something to do with the drinks they had or the way she felt when they touched briefly. Whatever it was, it had her feeling real frisky.

"Thanks for lunch. I really had a good time, and hopefully we can do this again."

"We definitely have to do it again sometime," Ashley said.

Taylor looked at the time and realized that she only had about thirty minutes before Trinity came home from school. That would be more than enough time for her to have some fun. She rushed into the house and up to her bedroom, undressing along the way. For the next twenty minutes, she relieved herself, using her sex toy. By the time her daughter came home, she had cleaned up and was making dinner.

~ ~ ~

"So how did your lunch go?" Karen asked when she came home from work. She had gotten mandated and had to do an extra shift. By the time she arrived, Ashley had breakfast and coffee waiting on the table. "Tell me everything."

"I'm not sure I should tell you. I don't know how you would react," she joked. They always joked with each other about stuff. Maybe that's one of the reasons why their relationship was going so strong now.

"Try me," she said, taking a sip of the hot coffee and eating a piece of toast.

"All right, she ran a fingernail up the inside of my thigh, under the table at the cafe."

"You're kidding me, right?" When Ashley didn't respond, her interest grew. She wanted to know everything else that took place at their little luncheon. "And how did you respond to that?"

"With pleasure. I slid a finger across her vagina to see if she was feeling what I was feeling. To my surprise, she was. I think it's safe to say that she wouldn't mind having that threesome with us."

"Just the thought of another woman touching you has turned me on. I think we should do something fun this morning before you have to go to work."

"Well, in that case," Ashley said, stuffing a piece of bacon down her throat. "Follow me so I can give you one of my famous lap dances, but let's be quick."

Karen grabbed her cup of coffee and headed upstairs behind her girl. Ashley pulled her nightgown over her head as she walked into their bedroom. Her body was thick and flawless. Her titties were nice and perky, her stomach wasn't flat, but it wasn't big either. She didn't have stretch marks or anything like that, which Karen loved about her.

"How you want it, baby?" Karen asked, pulling out her twelve-inch, strap-on dildo. "From the front, or back?" She gave her ass a slap so hard that it jiggled like a wave of water.

"You know how I like it," Ashley said, bending over the edge of the bed.

Karen stepped up behind her, positioning the dildo up to her hole, and slowly slid it in inch by inch. Ashley's moans started out low, but once Karen sped up the pace, they instantly became louder. Her pussy was taking every bit of the rubber dick. That was one of the other things that she loved about her girl.

"Oh shiiiittt, baby, I'm about to cum."

Karen started pounding her pussy even harder. They both were sweating profusely, even though the heat was on low. Ashley came all over the rubber dildo, then Ashley ate Karen's pussy until she came in her mouth.

"Wow, I guess we should both take a shower together," Karen said afterward.

"You go ahead. I'm going to take a nap."

"Suit yourself," Karen said, heading in the bathroom.

By the time Karen finished, Ashley was on the bed, sound asleep. She let her rest while she cleaned up the house.

SEVEN

"Monroe, can you give me a hand with this patient," the nurse asked one of the inmate porters.

He stopped playing cards and walked over to the room to assist her with helping the patient get to the bathroom. He wasn't trying to walk, so they had to help him into a wheelchair, then rolled him in. As they waited for him to finish, the nurse did something unexpectedly. She pretended like she dropped her ID on the floor and bent down to pick it up, giving Monroe a clear view of her panty line. At first, he didn't pay her any mind until she made a comment about the floor being sticky.

"I'm going to clean the bathroom in a few minutes," he said, turning around just in time to see what she was doing. His eyes almost popped out of his head when he saw how round her ass was.

Nurse Anna had been working there for a long

time. You couldn't even tell that she was forty-seven years old. She looked more like thirty-five. At five foot six and 141 pounds, with a golden white complexion, dark brown hair, perky 38 DD breasts, and the ass of a black woman, Anna was beautiful. She probably had the best body in the whole prison for a white female.

"Are you done?" she asked the patient. He nodded his head. "Okay, you have to stand up so I can wipe you, okay?"

Monroe passed her the wipes. When she grabbed the pack, she purposely rubbed her index finger over the back of his hand. If he didn't get the hint before, he damn sure was starting to get it now. He needed to be sure though.

"On three, we're going to lift him up," she told him. "One, two, three."

They helped the patient up, Monroe taking the bulk of his weight while Anna wiped him clean. After she finished and put a new pull-up on, together they sat him back down in the wheelchair. Monroe pushed him back to his bed, and they helped him sit back on it. In the midst of it, Anna's ass brushed his hand. It was really soft.

"Excuse me," Monroe said, respectfully.

"You didn't do anything. That was on me."

She gave him a wink before walking out of the room. Monroe was stunned by her sudden boldness. He knew she was a flirt, but what she was doing was borderline PREA status. He still didn't know if he should act on it or not. He needed more confirmation, and boy, would it come later on that evening.

All the other nurses had gone back to their assigned stations, leaving only Anna and Amanda because they were assigned to the nurses' station. Monroe went back to the isolation room to get the patients' water containers. When he walked out of the room, Anna was coming into the small hallway. As he was removing his mask, Anna slid in between him and the stand, this time making her ass brush up against his dick. It actually felt like she made her ass cheeks jump. However, this time there was no mistaking what she was doing.

"Damn," he said in a low tone.

"What was that?" she replied, sliding to the side as if nothing just happened. "Keep your mouth shut and it will get better. But if you say anything to anybody, I will deny it, and you will go to the hole. Are we clear on that?"

"I don't know what you're talking about."

Anna smiled in confirmation, then stepped out of the area. She went back to the nurses' station to finish prepping for her medical treatment line. Monroe started walking his one-on-one patient back and forth down the hall, trying to get him tired.

"They just called block trash. Do you want me to take it?" Howard asked.

He was a weirdo that just got paroled and was going home soon. Even though he was kind of a good guy, he would constantly try to do too much, and it pissed some people off.

"You or Stud can take it. I'm walking him."

Howard gathered all the trash and threw it in the big bin that was in the closet. He asked the officer to write him a pass so he could take it around to the trash receptacle.

"Thank you!" Howard said, pushing the bin out.

Monroe continued walking Brawny until eight o'clock, when he started showing all the signs of being tired. He asked Amanda to change him for the last time so he could lay him down. After he got changed, Monroe placed him in the bed with the sheet over his face because that's the only way he could sleep. That was all she wrote. Brawny went straight to sleep.

"Y'all can go back if you want," Monroe told the other porters.

They gathered up all their stuff and headed back to their housing units. Monroe wiped down the doorknobs and other things that people had been touching all day. Once he was finished, he sat in the room watching the basketball game. The infirmary officer and the rover walked by doing their evening count, then went and sat down because they were ready to go home.

Anna walked out of the nurses' station and headed into the back toward the staff break room. Monroe got up and walked that way.

"Ms. A," he yelled out. "Can you open the closet for me?"

He purposely had locked the door earlier when he was cleaning because he wanted to get her in the back. This was his chance to put it all to the test. If he was wrong, he would be going straight to the hole and probably getting transferred for assaulting a staff member. She unlocked the door for him.

"Thank you," he said, making sure the guards weren't watching them, then squeezed her ass.

His heart was racing the whole time, waiting for her to slap the shit out of him or call the guards, but none of that never happened. She just walked away smiling. That was the start of something special, and he promised himself that he wouldn't do anything stupid to jeopardize it.

EIGHT

"Hi, Daddy!"

"Hey, baby girl! How is my little princess doing?" Steve said, FaceTiming his daughter.

He went down to the naval base that was located in South Philadelphia, so it would look like he was on a ship somewhere. Since he was a lieutenant commander of a ship, he had no problem pulling it off. What he was hoping was that he could fool his wife.

Lately he had been noticing a different mood swing from Taylor. He had come to the assumption that she was mad that he was always gone and it was taking a toll on their marriage. If he only knew that she knew about his other family, he would stay away.

"Me and Mommy are going shopping in the morning to get me a new doll. Daddy, when are you coming home? I miss you."

Trinity kept going on and on about everything

going on. On one hand, Steve was laughing because here his ten-year-old was acting like she was still a baby. On the other hand, he felt bad about not being able to tell her that she had a little brother. He talked to her for a few more minutes. When he tried to talk to Taylor, she made up some excuse that she wasn't feeling well and that she needed to lie down.

"Okay, I'll let you go. I will be able to sneak out of here next week. How about you plan something special for the three of us, and then later I can give you something special?"

Taylor wanted to say something smart, but she didn't want to spoil what she had planned for him when he came home. She had paid someone to hack into his phone and upload photos of his other family to her laptop so she could confront him about it. She was hoping he would try to lie so she could proceed with filing for a divorce. If he told her the truth, she would try to get over it for the sake of their daughter and move on. Taylor kind of blamed herself. She couldn't have any more children and thought that's why it happened.

"Whatever," she smirked.

They talked for another two minutes, and then Taylor ended the call so she could take a nice hot bath. She turned on some music at a low volume while she lit scented candles and poured oils into the water. With so much going on in her life, this was what she needed right now.

She eased her way into the warm water. Leaning her head back and closing her eyes, Taylor let the sounds of Beyoncé soothe her body. For some strange reason, her mind drifted to the luncheon she had with Ashley and the chemistry she felt when they touched. The more she thought about it, the more she could feel her pussy jumping.

Without even thinking twice about it, Taylor's hand made its way down to the most sensitive part of her body. Soon as she touched her clit, it felt like she was going to explode. She flicked it a couple of times before sticking a finger deep inside her hole. When one finger wouldn't do the trick, she stuck two more inside. With her left hand caressing her pussy, her right hand grabbed her left breast and squeezed her nipple. She lifted it up to her mouth and began sucking on it. Beyoncé had ended, and now H.E.R.'s "Focus" was serenading her through the surround sound.

"Mmmmmm," she moaned, sucking on her breast harder. The harder she sucked, the more turned on she became. "Ohhh my God, Ashley, do it faster, baby."

She didn't even realize that she had just mentioned Ashley's name until she came in the water. The orgasm was hard and long. When her eyes popped opened, most of the candles had melted down and the water wasn't warm anymore.

"Damn, girl, you tripping," she mumbled to herself. "You need to get you some before you do something stupid."

Taylor hopped out of the tub, dried herself off with one of the plush towels, and then checked on

Trinity. After checking on her daughter, she got in bed. Her mind kept playing back to that touch and the powerful orgasm she just got finished having. Boy, was it powerful!

"What has gotten into me?" were the last words she said before drifting off to sleep.

~ ~ ~

Steve grabbed a drink and met Gina in the bedroom. She was sitting at her vanity desk, straightening her hair. He stood there staring at her. She looked good even when she wasn't dressed up. It finally hit him that Taylor was nothing like Gina. She had more going for her, and that wasn't counting all the money she and her brother had. If there was a person that he could see himself being with for the rest of his life, it would be her. He walked up behind Gina and kissed the back of her head.

"Hey, beautiful, wanna fool around a bit?"

Gina giggled like a little girl who just received a kiss from her crush. She turned around toward Steve and acted like she was surprised.

"I'm trying to do my hair, now leave me alone."

"I'll leave you alone," he said, dropping down to his knees in front of her.

She was wearing a silk nightgown that he slowly lifted up to her thighs. Gina's pussy was on fire, throbbing for attention. She quickly removed it the rest of the way. Her titties were the size of ripe grapefruits, and her nipples were hard as rocks. He tickled each one with the tip of his tongue.

"Damn, you got me so fucking wet," Gina moaned, rubbing her clit, then sticking her finger in his mouth so he could taste her sweet nectar.

She took one of her titties and placed it into her mouth, then started sucking on her nipple. That drove him crazy. Steve stood up and got undressed with the speed of lightning, and stood over Gina as she sat on the chair with her legs spread open. He then ripped off the thong she was wearing, pulling her forward in the chair so he could go to work on her pussy. Five minutes later, he was bringing her to a thunderous orgasm.

"This what you want, huh?" he whispered.

"Shut up and eat," she moaned.

He stood her up from the chair and bent her over the vanity table, plowing into her with force causing her to scream out in pleasure and pain. She thought he was trying to rip through her pussy and come out her mouth, as deep and hard as he went. He was killing the pussy.

"Ssss-awwww," Gina gasped, sucking in air through clenched teeth. He slid deeper inside her tight hole, trying to touch her stomach literally. "Ohhh shit, I'm about to cum. Faster, harder."

He eagerly accommodated her request as he also felt an orgasm approaching. They both came together to electrifying orgasms, but Gina wasn't done yet. She needed more after being deprived all day of her baby father. She just wanted him to fuck her until she couldn't be fucked anymore. That's exactly what he did until the wee hours of the morning.

Nine

"Monroe, are you and Ingles going to work?"
Officer Jankoski asked, looking over the wall. She was talking to someone on the phone as she spoke to him.

She was pulled off her block to work on M1 today because they wanted one of the trainees to experience what it was like to work the medical block. Karen didn't mind it at all. In fact, she wanted to work a regular block this shift so she could start some more trouble.

"Yeah, we're going."

"Okay, before you go I have something for you to give the nurse. Just tell her it's from me, and she will know what to do with it."

"I got you," Monroe replied, starting to get ready for work.

Even though he didn't want to work today, he had to go in. They still hadn't hired any more workers yet, so they were working a lot of hours.

Ingles and Monroe did most of the work because Howard acted like he didn't know what to do. Everyone was getting tired of his stupidity, but no matter what they said to try to help him, it never seems to get through his big-ass head.

Soon as he was done getting ready for work, he signed out on the tracking sheet that sat on the officer's desk and got his pass and the paper for the nurse from officer Jankoski, and then he and Ingles headed over to the infirmary. There were a bunch of new patients that had been committed, lying around waiting to see the doctor. Because it was Friday, whoever didn't get released today would be stuck there until Monday. That meant more work for just the three of them to do. They had some help from one of the morning shift porters, but he couldn't help them every day. Their boss was supposed to get a new worker sometime next week, then maybe they would be able to get a day off.

Soon as he got to work, Monroe filled the Cambros with ice water and refilled the cups. This was the task he performed every day before anything else.

"Good afternoon," he said to a couple of the nurses that walked past as he was dust mopping the floor.

They had arrived early for a meeting in the staff break room. They usually had it once every two weeks, but due to situations beyond their control, they hadn't had one in a couple of months. So as you can see, this was a meeting that was long overdue, and mandatory. Lately a lot of shit had been getting out of control in medical, and management needed to address some of those issues.

"What's up?" Amanda said. She was the first one to speak.

"What's up, Monroe?" Renata said.

Renata was one of the nurses going through a certain change in her life. By change, I mean she hadn't always been a female. She grew up as a man until she was around ten. That is when she realized how attractive she was to the same sex.

Her family didn't approve of the sudden change and kicked her out of the house. Renata ended up staying at her cousin's place.

A couple of months later, after reconciling with them, she moved back home with her parents. Her father, who was the most disappointed, welcomed her with open arms, even though he still felt some kind of way about her transition. His own reason for having a son in the first place was for the son to live out his dream and play football or basketball.

"How's the book coming along?" Amanda asked.

"It's coming," Monroe replied. "I have been working night and day to make my deadline. If I stay on course, it should be ready by next month."

"That's good. Let me know when it's in stores so I can go buy my copy and you can autograph it."

"Will do," Monroe told her as she hurried along to get to her meeting. She didn't want to be the last person that got there.

A few minutes later, Anna came strolling in

wearing her usual tight scrubs. Today she had on gray ones that fit her body like latex gloves. They were so tight, that if you looked closely, you could see her pussy lips poking through them.

"How you doing, Ms. A?"

"Hey," she smiled, and kept it pushing.

Monroe finished what he was doing, then sat down at the table with Brawny. He was sitting there enjoying himself, eating an apple. Howard walked in with his ripped up file folder around three minutes before they stopped movement for shift change, like he always did. He placed his folder on the shelf and then walked into one of the patient's rooms to watch television. This was his normal routine, until someone said something slick to him. Then he would walk around pretending like he was working.

Monroe liked picking with him, so he could see his reaction. Once he started talking shit, it was hard to stop him. The only way he would stop was if one of the nurses was around. He played the innocent, quiet type whenever they were in the vicinity. Ingles went upstairs to collect the trash from the offices.

"Howard, can you watch Brawny so I can do the laundry?"

"You want me to do it?"

"No, I got it," he told him, heading toward the closet. Howard sat down with Brawny and started doing his puzzle.

Fifteen minutes later, Monroe was still doing laundry when all the staff came storming out of the room. As they walked past, he could tell that it wasn't a pleasant meeting. Their faces said it all. Anna walked by the closet and gave him a half smile.

Once everyone had left the break room, Anna came back to the closet as Monroe was just finishing up with the laundry. She didn't come in, but stood by the door.

"Can you hand me one of those water containers, please?" When he turned around to grab the container, she squeezed his ass. "That was payback from what you did to me," she smirked, talking about the other day when he did the same thing to her.

"You're crazy," he replied, handing her the pitcher. "Where are you working at today?"

"I'm on C2. I'll see you later. When I come back over here, we have to talk. Are you still going to be here?"

"Yeah, I'm staying today."

Anna left to get some work done, leaving Monroe there wondering what she wanted to talk about. He saw Carla and gave her the note that Officer Jankoski gave him. He made sure he wasn't seen giving it to her because people tended to get the wrong idea about things. She read the note, looked at Monroe, and then walked out of medical in a hurry.

~ ~ ~

Karen was sitting in the fitness room waiting when Carla walked in. She had a smile on her face that lit up any room and made Karen melt at the thought of being near her.

"Why did you give a note to an inmate instead

of just calling me?" she asked, closing the door. "You know how much trouble that could have gotten us in?"

"I know I shouldn't be saying this, but I trust him more than I trust any of the staff. But you're right, I should have just called you."

"Don't worry about it. Anyway, what did you want to show me?"

"Sit here," Karen said, pointing to the massage chair.

There was a drink sitting in the cup holder, and a towel was covering the seat. Carla sat down in the chair and waited for further instructions. Karen turned the chair on, and it immediately went to work on her body. It was hitting the most sensitive part of her body: her pussy! She leaned back, closing her eyes, and let the chair do its magic. Every time the vibration got to her pussy, her clit jumped with anticipation. It felt like she had her toy at work with her.

Karen sat down next to her. She slid a hand down Carla's scrubs and started playing with her pussy while the vibrations did their job. Carla unbuttoned Karen's pants, slipped her own hand inside, and began fingering her pussy. Neither worried about being caught, due to it being count time. Plus, the door was locked. Karen's fingers sped up when she noticed Carla's facial expression.

"I'm about to cum."

"Me too," Karen moaned, feeling Carla's hand start to move faster in a circular motion.

They both came simultaneously, then sat there for a moment breathing heavily. Karen was the first to get up and fix her clothes, because she had a lot to fix. Carla watched in amazement how quickly she moved. The only thing Carla had to do was tie the drawstring on her scrubs, and she was complete.

"Time to get back to work," smiled Carla, opening the door. They both walked out together. Officer Smart was sitting at the 42nd Street desk. She just gave them a confirmation head nod and continued doing whatever it was she was doing.

"Ashley got my neighbor to open up a bit. So it will be four of us tomorrow night."

"Wow, I didn't think she would be able to do that. What about her husband?"

"What about him? He is out at sea, and she's here with their child. She has an itch that needs scratching just like any other person that has to be away from their spouse for a long period of time," Karen stated.

Even though she and Ashley lived together, they still did their thing on the side. The only thing Karen asked was that they both agreed on who they did it with. So far it had been nothing but fun.

"Well I guess I will see y'all heifers tomorrow. Maybe I'll stop in Dickson City and pick up something special, if you know what I mean." Carla winked.

"Grab something for me too."

Carla smiled and flicked her the middle finger. Karen mouthed the word "When?" and continued down the hall.

TEN

Monroe sat in the dayroom playing poker with a few guys that he lived on the block with. They had a cool officer that didn't care about anything but doing his eight hours and going home. He left work early that day because technically he was off and he was trying to catch a show that he watched every Wednesday.

Although he was losing right now, he still was betting like crazy. The previous hand, he bet a large amount trying to make people fold. Only one person stayed in the hand, and he had a pair of aces. Monroe had two kings and a possible spade flush. The flop was a queen of spade, four of spade, and ten of diamond. The next card that flipped was another ten. Monroe had his spade flush.

"I check," Monroe said, thinking he was baiting the other guy in.

"Check is good."

The next card that turned was an ace of heart,

giving the guy the highest full house on the board. Monroe sat there for a moment wondering if his flush was a winner or not. He looked around to see if anyone was giving the man's hand away. Testing the waters, he made a small bet.

"I'll bet ten chips."

"I call your ten, and I'm all in," the man said, putting the rest of his chips in. Since he only had three more chips left, Monroe snap called him. "I have a boat."

When he showed his pair of aces, Monroe shook his head. He had been set up this time. Usually, it would be him doing the baiting, but this time he was the baited.

"Good shit, bro," Monroe said, giving him his props. "I knew you had something, I just didn't know what."

The next hand he went all in without even looking at his hand, and lost again. He never had a chance this time. He got up from the table and headed back to his bunk. One of the other men in his cube was making some banana pudding and asked him if he wanted some. Monroe turned it down and sat on his bunk to watch television.

"The phone list is out," the officer yelled out. "And get off my tier; white shirts are coming."

Everyone respected him because he never acted like a prick, so they moved off the range, into the bathroom area or their cubes. The lieutenant and a captain walked into the block, signed the book, and headed upstairs to check on the next block. The officer called upstairs to inform his colleague that she was getting some company. By this time it was getting close to count time, so Monroe checked the kiosk then sat on his bunk and tried to finish reading a book called *Supreme and Justice* by Ernest Morris. The more he read, the more his thoughts went back to the conversation that he and Anna had right before he left.

She told him how much she was starting to like him and that she wished he wasn't in prison so they could try to build something. She also reminded him that nothing could really happen because she wasn't trying to lose her job. This was her only financial support. Her husband had been a deadbeat; that's why they were separated. She took care of their children by herself.

When she first met him, she knew he was something special. His whole demeanor said he didn't belong there. Just to make sure that her suspicions were right, she googled his name to see what she could find out about him. She was impressed by what she found out. She decided that he would be the one that she gave a chance. The only problem that they had was him being in prison. He was worth waiting for, and Anna would do what she needed to make sure he knew it.

"Monroe, are you watching *60 Days In*," his bunkie asked, snapping him out of his thoughts.

"Yeah," he said. "I'm a have to flip back and forth from the game and that. You know I gotta chase this money."

"You want some of this food?"

"Hell no! You know damn well I don't eat that shit." Monroe didn't eat like others. He only ate plain chicken soups, or fried chicken and rice.

"This shit is good, bro."

Monroe didn't respond. He just continued reading his book and listening to the rest of the people in his cube make fun of each other. Once the lights went out, he watched his television until he dozed off to sleep.

~ ~ ~

The next day when Monroe came to work, it seemed like everyone was in a panic. Somehow word had spread throughout the prison about someone being affected with the coronavirus disease, and now the prison was taking many precautions. The infirmary supervisor had all the workers scrubbing down everything with bleach.

Howard and Ingles were moving all the patients around, while Monroe swept and mopped the rooms. The nurses cleaned their own stations and the break room. All the K block workers were doing the same, trying to protect the patients living there. The person with the coronavirus-like symptoms was locked in one of the isolation rooms. No one could go in or out of there without wearing proper protective gear. They were taking this very seriously. The supervisor pulled all the workers into the dayroom to talk to them.

"Until we find out if this person tested positive or not, I don't want you guys going around gossiping about this, okay?"

"I mind my business, you know that," Howard was the first to say, getting scared.

"I shouldn't hear nothing about anyone saying that one of you opened your mouths about what's going on here," she said, the whole time looking at Ingles.

Stud had a way of running his mouth about everything he heard. He just reacted instead of thinking first, and then blamed it on the medication he took.

"Wh ... wh ... why you looking at me?" he asked, stuttering.

"If this gets out and I find out that it came from one of my porters, you will immediately be done here. This is a medical department only issue, and you shouldn't be talking about it."

They listened to the supervisor rant on and on for a few more minutes about how to prevent coming in contact with the virus, then went back to cleaning. Every hour someone was wiping down doorknobs and anything else people touched. The nurses were advised to wear gloves, and wash their hands every time they finished dealing with a patient, and so were the porters.

Monroe was walking Brawny while Stud helped Amanda change the linen on a patient's bed. Because he wasn't able to move around, he was always sweating, and the sheets would get soaked. He could, however, sit up to eat and drink, but that was about it. He even had trouble using the bathroom by himself.

Carla was carrying two huge boxes out of the pharmacy when one of them fell out of her hand. Monroe rushed over to give her a hand.

"I got it," he said, picking up the box.

"Thank you! Can you give these to Renata for

me?"

He dropped the boxes off at the nurse's station, then continued walking Brawny. Monroe had brought his tablet to work so Brawny could listen to it as he walked. It was just one of the nice things the workers usually did for him. In the summer, they would buy him sodas and ice cream from the stand when they took him to the yard. He would only walk around the track two times before getting tired. In the infirmary, though, he could walk for hours before showing any sign of tiredness.

"Trays are coming," the officer said, making his rounds.

"Here, sit Brawny down while I fill up the utensil box," Monroe said, passing him off to Howard. He walked to the back closet, but it was locked. Just when he was about to call the officer, Anna came walking through the door from K1. "What's up, Ms. A? Can you unlock this for me?"

"Sure!" she said, snapping her keys from her waist. "Anything else you need unlocked?"

Monroe looked to see if anyone was watching from the isolation rooms, then took two steps back into the closet and whipped out his dick.

"Can you unlock this?"

"Damn," was the only word that came out her mouth as she stood there staring at all ten inches of his thick anaconda.

You could see the sides of her mouthwatering up. Monroe stood there stroking himself in front of her while she continued to watch in amazement. Anna had never seen a dick that big in her life, except maybe when she enjoyed the occasional porn flick with her ex. On top of that, she had never been with a black guy either. As his hand went back and forth over the tip of his dick, Anna had to squeeze her legs together to keep her juices from leaking out into her panties.

"Would you like to touch it?"

Before she could come up with an answer, she noticed Howard coming down the hall, carrying trays in his hands.

"You want me to open the door for you," she

said, trying to warn Monroe to fix his pants. He caught on just in time as Anna opened the isolation door.

"Thanks," Howard replied.

"You're welcome," she told him, then gave Monroe a crazy look. She mouth the word *later* to him as she headed toward the nurses' station.

Monroe finished filling up the utensils then headed back over to help the other workers feed the patients. He hoped that he and Anna would be able to link up later when no one was around. He only had until ten to try to make something happen. He would not waste that chance if and when it presented itself. Unfortunately, that chance wouldn't come for either of them that night.

ELEVEN

The Red Carpet Motel just off the highway on Lackawanna Avenue was understaffed, overpriced, and excessively seedy. All the grim, peeling walls, off-white towels, and pot smoke and piss stench $70 a night could buy. They had decided not to use the Hilton this time because of the traffic coming in and out of the new Arcade across the street. Their rendezvous were supposed to be as secretive as possible.

Karen had arrived at the motel ahead of everyone else so she could get everything ready. Sitting cross-legged on the desk that she'd moved in front of her window, she slowly propped her digital camera on it. This was part of their game. They had recorded every session they had with each other in the last two years. It was kept on a flash drive that Karen kept safely secured in her safe at home.

She had yet to tell Taylor that she would be in

a sex video. She just hoped that she would at least try and have some fun. Knowing that they would be there in about twenty minutes, Karen had to hurry up and finish setting things up. She laid all the different sex toys on the bed, lit the scented candles, turned down the lights, and poured liquor into all the glasses. Once that was done she turned on the television and ordered a couple of lesbian porno movies.

By time Karen saw the headlights of Ashley's car pulling into the driveway, everything was ready to go. She opened the door to help them bring in the food.

"I thought we were going out to a club," Taylor smiled, stepping out of the car. "You got me all dressed up for nothing."

"Oh, trust me, it won't be for nothing," Carla replied, holding a tray of edible arrangements in her hand as she exited the passenger seat.

"Don't pay her lil freaky ass any mind," Karen chuckled. "She's just excited that we have to break in a new member of our crew."

"What kind of crew am I joining?"

"We are a secret society," Ashley began. "For the last year, it has been just the three of us. When me and you were having lunch the other day, I could feel a chemistry building between us. That's why I wanted to invite you to one of our outings. If what I was feeling is any kind of a sign of what's to come, then tonight is going to be a great time for all of us."

When they walked inside the room and Taylor saw all the sex toys on display and the movie that was playing on the flatscreen, she tried her best to hide the excitement she was feeling, but it wasn't working. She sat on the couch opposite the bed, watching the girls get comfortable.

"I guess this party can begin," Karen said, handing everyone a glass of liquor.

By the time everyone else was on their third drink, Taylor was still on her first and feeling tipsy already. She watched as Ashley sat her drink down, stood up, and started coming out of her dress. She was wearing a white crotchless, see-through panty-and-bra set. Karen sat on the bed making out with Ashley. Taylor couldn't believe what she was not only witnessing but was about to partake in. Her own panties became moist.

"Come over here." Ashley motioned for Taylor to join them on the king-size bed. She hesitantly stood up and slowly walked toward them. "Don't be nervous. We don't bite, unless you want us to."

Taylor sat on the edge of the bed as Ashley walked around and stood in front of her. By now Karen had Carla's legs in the air with her head in between them. Ashley didn't bother removing Taylor's dress. She knew how horny she was right now. Taylor instinctively raised her ass in the air as Ashley shoved her skirt up around her waist.

Ashley could hardly control herself as she slid her panties, a purple, silky thong, down her legs, leaving them dangling from one ankle. Taylor took hold of one of Ashley's hands and one by one, pulled her fingers into her mouth, sucking them one at a time.

"You have beautiful hands," she whispered.

"That was the first thing I noticed about you when we had lunch the other day."

Ashley watched her in amazement. She could tell the Molly Karen had placed in everyone's drink was starting to kick in, especially for Taylor. She took the hand she was sucking and pushed it down the center of her body, leaving a wide, moist trail. She planted Ashley's hand against her pussy and stared at her. Ashley took that as her cue and rubbed her hand over Taylor's pussy slowly, feeling the warm moisture that radiated from it. She then lowered her mouth between Taylor's thighs, licking the warm spaces between her splayed fingers.

Taylor shivered, and Ashley shyly spread her fingers, exposing the downy strip of her pussy lips. Sliding her tongue between them, she licked upward. Her taste changed from subtle to thick and sharp along this intimate geography. Taylor's clit, when Ashley reached it, was far softer than she imagined, but sensitive. Her thighs trembled each time her tongue passed over it.

"Oh shiiiittt, that feels so good," Taylor moaned.

Ashley raised slightly and leaned forward, resting her forehead against the upper swell of her breasts and slid two fingers inside Taylor as she pressed her thumb to her clit. She was tight, tighter than she expected, and her wetness slid around her fingers like warm water.

Taylor was tracing Ashley's shoulders with her fingers, carefully wedging one of her feet between their bodies, pressing the arch against the softness of her pussy. It was as warm as hers. She reached down and slid a finger inside to see if her foot was deceiving her. It wasn't! It felt so good that she began flicking her fingers over her clit, causing Ashley to squirm.

It caused Ashley's fingers to go faster. Taylor adjusted, spreading her legs wider. Ashley twisted her hand and arched her fingers upward, exploring the silky smoothness covering hard bone, the way her pussy curved.

"Does it feel good?"

"Yes," Taylor moaned, still fingering Ashley's pussy at the same time she was doing her.

Over on the other side of the bed, Karen had thrown on a strap-on and was fucking Carla doggy style while watching her girl please their new member. The dildo that Karen had attached to the strap on was the one that vibrated. She had it on high, and it had Carla begging for mercy. The faint scent of pussy could be smelled throughout the room, over the scented candles. It wasn't a bad smell though. In fact, it actually smelled like strawberries and cherries.

Ashley was trying to find the deepest, pulsating part of Taylor's body, though she was not quite sure that such a thing was possible. The opening of Taylor's pussy puckered around her fingers. Taking a deep breath, Ashley let her pinky slip inside of her. Slowly at first, she began to fuck her with her fingers, sliding them in to the third knuckle, then pulling back, then sliding back in.

There was a sound, a soft, squishy sound that Ashley hoped she would never forget. Taylor began rocking her hips, and she moaned, a high-pitched, squeaky moan that bordered on laughter. Her thighs were slick with sweat. Taylor was still fingering Ashley when she came, but never stopped her stroking. Ashley came a minute later.

"More," Taylor said tersely. "I need more."

She was so horny by now that she could have fucked anything that was in the vicinity of her pussy. Karen heard her request and immediately obliged. She stopped fucking Carla and hopped off the bed.

"Bend your ass over the bed," she ordered. Taylor saw the length of the vibrating dildo and damn near had another orgasm before it even touched her. "I got something for you."

Karen eased inside Taylor from behind, taking her time, then sped up the pace. She fucked her harder and faster with each stroke. She grabbed Taylor's ass and squeezed causing her moans to get louder.

"Yeesssss, oh shit!"

Karen was giving her all she could take, when

she screamed out from another thunderous orgasm. This one was by far more explosive than the one she had a few minutes ago, or anyone she had with her husband. He made her cum, but it wasn't anything like this. It made her think that he wasn't doing something right. She even wondered if a woman was a better pleaser than a man was.

Taylor glanced over to see Ashley and Carla in the 69 position, eating each other out. Carla's hands were handcuffed to the headboard, and Ashley was on top, feeding her pussy to Carla's awaiting mouth while she feasted on her swollen clit. Taylor felt her hormones activating again. She pushed Karen down on her back and started sucking the dildo as if it was a real dick.

"So you are a freak, huh?" Karen smirked, holding her head as it bobbed up and down. Her deep-throating was a work of perfection. She was damn near able to take in the whole ten inches. Karen bit down on her bottom lip at the sight of the way she sucked on that rubber dick. Soon as she felt herself about to cum, Karen pulled

Taylor's head up. "Ride it."

Taylor moved her body up and straddled the dildo. She lowered her pussy onto it and started bouncing up and down. The vibration from the dildo and Taylor's body made Karen bust in no time. Soon after, Taylor was having yet another orgasm.

For the next two hours, they took turns giving each other orgasm after orgasm. Taylor had never had so many in her life. It was like she was having an out-of-body experience. By the time she got home, it was going on four o'clock. The babysitter was asleep on the couch, and Trinity was asleep in her room. Taylor pulled out a blanket from the closet and placed it over the babysitter.

After covering up the sitter, she went up to her bedroom to get ready for a shower. By the time she took all of her clothes off, she was exhausted and never made it to the bathroom. She fell asleep butt naked, lying across her bed.

The next morning, when Taylor woke up, her body was aching, and she had a pounding headache. She didn't even want to get out of bed, but the smell of bacon and eggs had her stomach growling. Her pussy was so sore that when she went to the bathroom to pee, she realized that she was walking funny. Taylor threw on a robe to cover her naked body, then went downstairs to see who was cooking breakfast. When she walked into the kitchen, Trinity and the babysitter were sitting at the table making a plate of food.

"Hey, Mommy, me and Megan made breakfast for you," Trinity said excitedly.

"You did?" Taylor said, sitting next to her at the table. She picked up a piece of bacon and shoved it in her mouth. She looked at Megan. "Thank you for taking care of my little munchkin last night for me."

"No problem. I love watching her. She is so perfect," Megan stated. "Well I have to get home and clean up before my mom gets home. If you need me, just call or text me."

Megan got up and left. Taylor finished eating breakfast with her daughter; then they both took showers and got dressed. She wanted to spend the day with her baby. As she was putting on her sneakers, she received a text message from an unknown caller. It was a video message. She sat down on the couch.

What Taylor saw when she played the video made her heart skip a beat. It was a video of her and the other women engaging in their sexual festivities. Whoever sent that video wanted to see how she would react. In as if on cue, Taylor sent a response.

```
TO: 570-872-4103
WHO THE HELL IS THIS AND
WHY DID YOU SEND THAT TO ME?
```

She waited a few minutes to see if they would reply. As she was about to call Ashley and Karen, she finally received a message, but it wasn't what she expected.

```
FROM: 570-872-4103
I WANT $5,000.00 IN CASH BY MONDAY
OR THAT VIDEO GOES VIRAL. NO COPS!
```

"What's wrong, Mommy?" Trinity asked, seeing tears begin to form in her mother's eyes as she stared at her iPhone.

"Nothing! I'm okay," Taylor lied, wiping her eyes. "Go get your jacket so we can go."

She waited for Trinity to go upstairs, then texted Karen and Ashley, sending them the message and video she just got. Ashley was the first to call her back.

"Are you serious? Who would do such a thing?" she said as soon as Taylor answered.

"That's what I want to know. Did anyone else know that we were going to that hotel?"

"No. We never used that place before. I tried reaching Karen, but she's at work. Her phone is in the car, and I'm not going to call the prison, because they record calls."

"We have to figure something out. I can't let my family find out about this," Taylor complained.

Although she knew about Steve's infidelity, she couldn't let him or any of their family members find out about hers. This would mess up everything she had planned for him. She was especially worried about her daughter finding out. That was not an option. Mistakes were made, and lines were crossed on both ends, but she still had the upper hand as long as this didn't get out. Right now she had to figure out who was behind this, and if she was willing to pay the money or not. They were only asking for a small amount, and it would stop a huge catastrophe.

"Just pay the money, Tay," Ashley said, calling her by her nickname. "Where do you have to send it?"

"They didn't say anything yet. I didn't ask until I talked to you and Karen."

"As soon as Karen calls me back, I'll fill her in on what's going on so we can all sit down and figure this out together. Don't worry, we will handle this before they try to put it online. You're part of the secret society now, and we take care of our own."

Once she ended the call, Taylor kept her promise and took her daughter out shopping. The whole time, she was trying to figure out who was behind this blackmail.

TWELVE

"You good, cellie?" Monroe's cellmate asked.

"Yeah, I'm Gucci, bro," he replied, trying to hide his excitement. He swore never to tell him or anyone else about his new situation. Nothing was gonna fuck up what he had going on.

Monroe had been creeping around with Anna for the last couple of days. Every chance they had to be alone, they would get a few quick feels in here and there. The best chances they had were when he helped her change Brawny in the bathroom. As she changed him, Monroe would squeeze her breasts, or stick his hand down her pants, trying to play with her ass or pussy. Anna would get so turned on, then get mad because he couldn't finish what he started. They finally got the chance to christen their relationship one Sunday evening.

They had begun night yard, and all the workers went outside, leaving Monroe there to clean and watch the two remaining patients that couldn't go. Since it was the weekend, there weren't that many nurses on schedule, which made what they wanted to do that much easier. The guard that worked was Anna's cousin, so she let Anna do just about anything she wanted.

Normally, the inmate workers weren't allowed to go in the staff break room without the officer, but today was different. After making sure the patients were sleeping, Monroe went into the break room, with Anna trailing closely behind.

"Listen, I'm going to quit this job once you come home, and we're going to leave this nut-ass state, only if you want too!" Anna said, getting comfortable in one of the chairs.

"Of course," Monroe replied, trying to hide his excitement and wondering what life would be like with this white woman.

Anna stood up and pulled down her pants to unveil a pink shoestring thong. Monroe knew her pussy was fat, but when he saw it poking through the fabric of her panties, his dick damn near popped out of his pants.

"Wow, you're so fucking sexy," he said staring at her body. All this time, he thought she was wearing a girdle, but it was tights. Anna had the perfect body.

"You really like it," she asked while pulling her thong to the side, showing off her fat, hairless pussy. Her lips looked like they were swollen from some type of injection, but they were all natural.

"Hell yesss!" Monroe said quickly.

"Well come show me how much you like it then."

He dropped to his knees and buried his face in her pussy. Anna's pussy smelled so good. He moaned, and so did she. Monroe was an expert in eating pussy. He could make a woman cum within two minutes of his tongue touching their clitoris. He used to brag to her about it all the time, and now here he was giving it to her firsthand.

He flicked his tongue over her clit as he gripped her super-soft ass cheeks. Anna felt like she had died and gone to heaven.

"Oh my Gaaaawwwwd," she hissed as she held on to the table she was leaning on with one hand, and his head with the other. "Fuck.. . You... Knowwwwwww howwwwww ... To eat a pussy, don't youuuuu."

"I told you to do your homework on me before you start talking shit."

"I'm cumming," Anna hissed with lustful difficulty while shivering in wild convulsions.

Monroe ran his tongue deep into her pussy hole and back to her clit as he squeezed and spread her ass cheeks apart. It felt so good that she could hardly keep her balance and fell back on the table. Monroe's tongue never deterred from its mission to make her have multiple orgasms.

"Ohhh shiiiittt..." she yelled out as he swallowed all she had to offer. He slurped, sucked and licked her clean.

"Hurry up and shove that dick up in this," Anna begged, finally getting the chance to see how it would feel to have some black inmate's dick all up in her. She turned around and bent over the table. "Put it in slowly. This is my first time having something so big."

Monroe wasn't ready to give her the dick yet. He pulled her thong to the side. Her white tan-lined ass was too perfect. He pulled them apart to see her hole. It was nice and light brown. The actual hole was a reddish-pink dot. Monroe licked it a couple of times nice and hard, sending chills throughout her body.

"Holy fuck! You're a beast," Anna grunted as soon as he stuck his tongue deep up her ass. That was also a feeling she'd never experienced. She had been used to the typical kind of fuck, but this was by far the best she'd ever had. "Fuuuck."

Monroe stood straight up. "You ready for this big shit that's all yours now?"

"Oh God, yes . . . and it is mine, right?"

"Hell yeah, all yours," Monroe replied as he shoved instead of gently guiding his dick into her dripping wet warm pussy. Anna closed her eyes and tried to take it, but it was too much.

"Shit . . . he'll rip meee!" she yelled as she tried to pull away, but Monroe held her hips and slammed away. Her pussy was hot and tight.

"Ahhhhh, your pussy feels so good," Monroe yelled out a bit too loudly. "Damn, my bad. I'm addicted to this shit already."

"It's . . . you . . . yours . . . baby," Anna tried to say, but the feeling of Monroe's dick was breathtaking.

Monroe pumped harder, his balls slapping her clit. Her reddish-pink ass was bouncing wildly all over the place. He spit on that delicious asshole of hers and slipped his thumb right inside. The feeling of her body being double penetrated sent her into a frenzy of orgasms. It seemed like they were coming one after the other as he beat her pussy up with his dick, and her ass with his thumb.

"Oh my Goshhhh, I love it in there too," she moaned naughtily. It was at that moment that she released her freaky side. If she knew back then what she knew now, she would have fucked a black man a long time ago. "Oh yeah, fuck my ass."

"Oh, is this really what you want, you little slut bitch?" Monroe grunted.

"Yeesssss, babbbby. I love to be talked to dirty. Pull my hair; I'm your fucking whore. Fuck your bitch," Anna moaned. Monroe had really made her freaky side emerge.

He was wailing away, fucking her like a porn star. She was a true slut with an appetite for sex, and Monroe was the solution to her problem.

"I'm about to bust," he said while thrusting as hard as he could muster with a new energy. Smacking noises and moans filled the room.

"Ahhhhh, ahhhhghh," they both yelled as they came together. There was so much semen between the both of them that the thick fluids started spilling out over the table and floor before Monroe even pulled out.

"Fuck," Anna said, catching her breath. "That was the best five minutes I ever had." Monroe didn't respond to what she said.

He pulled out and stared at her wet ass and

dripping pussy. She turned around to face his dick, dropped down, and sucked him clean. It miraculously began to get him excited again. Anna noticed it was still semi-erect and touched it.

"Wow, baby . . . you're still hard as a rock!" she said in amazement. Monroe was just as shocked as she was, but eager and ready. Anna checked her watch. "Fuck me in the ass real quick before we have to leave."

She took off her shoes, then pulled her pants completely off, leaving them on the floor. Anna knew she was taking a chance by taking them off, but was so horny that she didn't care. She was feeling herself. Monroe sat down in the chair like she motioned for him to do.

"Get my asshole wet?" she asked excitedly. Monroe licked her asshole as she bent over in front of him. He then used some of that thick hanging cum from her pussy and pushed it up in her ass with his fingers. "I'm ready, baby."

Monroe sat back in the chair as she pulled her ass cheeks apart. He aimed his dick at her opening, and she slowly tried to sit on it. It was too thick to enter her tight hole, so he spit on his fingers and lubed her opening some more.

"Ohhh shiiiittt, he's too big. I don't think I can take it," she yelled as he grabbed her hips and eased her down.

Within minutes, Monroe was ten inches deep inside her. She started to bounce on it like a pro. Her ass felt so good to him. It just bounced and wobbled every time she came down on his dick. He reached under her shirt and lifted Anna's bra so he could squeeze her soft breast. She was getting used to it now. Her hole had expanded to the size of his girth.

"Yesss, baby, squeeze my titties," she moaned softly, slamming herself harder on his dick.

"Your asshole is so tight. Damn it feels good."

"Hurrryyyyy ... up ... and .. . cummm," was all she could stutter. "We have to go before someone catches us."

That's what he did, too! He shot his load deep inside her. When he pulled his dick out, a small puddle came with it.

"I'm speechless," Monroe stated, pulling up his pants.

"Good, that's how I like to leave people," Anna said, hurriedly putting her thong and scrubs back on. He gave her a seductive stare like he was undressing her all over again. "No, baby, we can't do it no more. At least not today."

"I know. I was just playing. Let's get out of here before someone misses us," Monroe said, opening the windows to air it out, then heading for the door.

"Wait!" Anna said, grabbing his arm. "I don't usually do that, so don't think any differently of me, okay?"

"Baby, I will never judge you," he replied, giving her a kiss on the lips, then walking out of the break room ahead of her. She waited a few seconds then did the same.

THIRTEEN

Steve and Gina lay in bed watching the news. They were trying to see if there were any new updates on the coronavirus that was spreading throughout the United States. So far it had hit a couple of states. Last night one of the NBA stars was diagnosed with it, causing them to shut down the league temporarily.

"This is so fucked up," Steve said, sipping on a cup of coffee. "They may cancel the league for the rest of the year because of this virus."

"I mean, what can you do? Right now, no one is safe unless you simply stay away from everyone. We can't even go out of the country right now because of flight restrictions."

"That's why I need to get home and make sure my daughter is alright."

"You mean make sure your wife is alright?" Gina said with a disappointed look on her face. "Why the fuck can't you just call them?"

"Look, I can't do this with you right now, okay? You knew what you were getting into when you decided to have this baby."

"You mean when we decided to have this fucking baby. I didn't lie down and fuck myself, and I damn sure didn't cum in myself," Gina snapped. "We did this to-fucking-together. Stop trying to blame everyone else and take responsibility for your own actions. I wish you would have told me that you were married before we fucked."

"I told you that I'm working on the details of the divorce. Soon as it is all worked out, we can move on with our lives. You have to trust me. Do you?"

Gina was lost for words. She didn't know if she should trust him or not. Because she loved him and loved their son, she wanted to make it work.

"Yes, I told you before that I trust you, but me and your son need you around too," Gina replied, tears coming down her face. Why can't you just bring your daughter here?

"Because I have to explain to her why we're getting a divorce, and see how she reacts," he lied.

The truth was Taylor would never allow her daughter to see Gina or her son. When they first talked about his infidelity, he promised that he'd never do it again. That was all a lie. He and his crew hadn't been back to the ship in over six months. His wife thought that he was out to sea, but he was definitely still on land. Just not in Scranton where she was.

"Well how about you take him with you to see his sister, and I get a little break from watching him for a weekend. Then you can tie up any loose ends with your soon-to-be ex-wife."

"You know I can't do that either," he told her, getting up to get dressed. He was going back home today to surprise Taylor. "When I get back, you can do whatever you wish, and I will stay home with Steve Jr. How's that sound?"

"That sounds great, but if you want me to be happy until you get back, then I think you should leave me with something to remember you by,"

Gina said in a seductive manner.

"Let's see what I can do," Steve replied, walking toward her. "I guess I better hurry up before Stevie wakes up and cockblocks me."

"Shut up and fuck me," she laughed, sliding her hand down his chest and down his sides as she pressed her hips into his.

Gina moved to the edge of the bed and stood up in front of him. She kissed him hard. Her tongue slipped out, parting his mouth, intertwining with his. Steve let her take control. She grabbed his wrist and plunged his hand down her shorts, between her legs, moving aside her panties so that his fingers glided against her pussy. Slippery hot, she sighed heavily in his mouth as she pressed his fingers against her clit, grinding herself against his hand.

Steve stroked her pussy until she started to squirm and pant into his mouth. Gina reciprocated the feeling by sticking her hand inside his pants, wrapping her hand around his dick that was now fully awake, and stroking it nice and slow.

"Shit!" Steve backed up and looked at how beautiful she was.

"What?"

"Nothing," he replied.

Gina removed her clothes and leaned back on the mattress, situating her ass and beckoning him to come and get it. Steve's dick was at full attention by now. She grabbed it, positioning it between her legs.

"Just fuck me," she said, urging him on.

Steve's breath was sweet, smelling like mouthwash, as he knelt down in front of her. His fingers opened her up, and he began tonging her clit. Gina felt herself melting, legs going weak. This was the effect he had over her body, and she loved it. Steve leaned back, pulling her onto the floor with him, and slithered his dick into her wet pussy, smooth and wide.

Gina was lost in the exotic world that she would go into every time they had sex. He fucked her deep and hard, his fingers pulling her ass cheeks apart. He slipped one in her ass, sending tiny jolts of pleasure throughout her body, especially her pussy. She pulled herself astride to take him even farther in, gripping as she raised herself to the tip, then bouncing down, feeling every inch of him smooth and hot. Gina lifted her ass and turned toward his legs for the reverse cowgirl style. The view of her ass drove him crazy.

Slow, wet, and warm, Steve rocked her, up and down, teeter-totter, over and over. He fucked her so good that when she came, it flowed out like a water faucet. Now he needed to get his off before he left. He flipped her over on her back, threw her legs up in the air, and pounded away. Gina's breasts bounced up and down with every thrust he gave her.

"I'm about to cum again, baby. Harder, fuck me harder."

Steve tried to do just that too. He dug deep into her hole like he was trying to make his dick pop out of her mouth. Gina took everything he could dish out.

"I want another baby," she moaned, causing Steve to stop in mid-stroke. It was like his dick went limp from hearing the words *another baby*! He picked Gina up off of him like she weighed twenty pounds.

"What's wrong?" she asked, puzzled.

"What did you just say?"

"I said I want another baby. If you really want to marry me, then put another baby inside me before you go back to that bitch," Gina stated firmly, not backing down from what she wanted.

She was giving him an ultimatum, that either he would agree to or not. Gina was very wealthy, so she wasn't trying to get any money from him. In fact, she was willing to take care of him. Steve looked at her like she had just given him an STD or something.

"Do not call the mother of my child a bitch again," Steve snapped. "I would never let her call you out, so don't do it to her. This is not the time to be talking about another baby. I told you before, that there's too much going on in my life right now. Once I've taken care of my other arrangements, then we can talk about that. Not before."

Gina was pissed that he was talking to her like that. As much as she wanted to sit there and argue, Gina knew it wouldn't get anywhere. She was about to say something just so she could have the last word, but their son started crying.

"Aren't you gonna say bye to Stevie before you go?"

Steve never answered her question with words. He walked out of the room, kissed his son on the forehead, and then headed out the door. Instead of flying back home to make it look good, he drove the car that Gina had given him. He took the time he drove back to Scranton to figure out what he was going to do before it all blew up in his face.

FOURTEEN

Karen left for work early the next morning. Which, if you were traveling through the city and wanted to avoid being late due to the COVID-19 testing you had to take every time you got to work, it meant you had to leave a bit earlier. The governor of Pennsylvania had declared a state of emergency and closed all the schools, amongst other businesses, because there were now twenty-seven confirmed cases and counting.

She hadn't gotten much sleep thanks to the news she received the other night about someone trying to blackmail her friend. Taylor had been taking it kind of hard even though she didn't want to admit it, wondering who was behind it. Her husband surprised them by coming home for the weekend, and she didn't want him finding out about it. Karen had informed her that she would do everything she could to help find the person that was responsible for this.

Last night when they all talked about the situation, Karen advised Taylor to pay the money and she would be right there with her when it happened, to make sure nothing happened to her. Now they were just waiting for whoever was behind it to call with a meeting spot.

When Karen arrived at work, the line had already begun to form. It was like everybody had read her mind to get there extra early. She parked in the lot and quickly rushed over to the sally port. After getting tested and coming up negative, she went inside, clocked in, and headed to her assigned block.

"You have forty-seven inmates on, twenty-five off, and one bed on hold," Officer Williams said, passing her the block keys and radio. "The OC spray and cuffs are in the top drawer."

"Okay! Anything else I should know about?"

"Not really. The block has been quiet for the most part. The inmates that signed up for the library, I already made their passes, so they're ready to go."

"Well, I will see you tomorrow," Karen said, clipping the keys on.

"Take care!" Officer Williams replied, leaving the block.

No sooner than Karen sat down after making her first rounds, did Sargent Oswald walk on the block. She was new to the prison and was already making a name for herself. She was one tough son of a bitch that no one wanted to cross. She had grown up in Brooklyn, then moved to Enon, Pennsylvania, about two years ago. She was a military vet, with numerous accommodations. She fought in a couple of wars.

She took on the job at SCI-Retreat as a correction officer and became a sergeant in no time. Many people believed that she fucked her way to that position. They heard many rumors that were never confirmed. When she found out that the prison was closing, she decided to transfer to one that was still within the same traveling distance, if not closer to her house. That's why she chose to come to Waymart.

"How's it going, Officer Jankoski?" Sargent Oswald asked, signing the book then taking a seat in the chair next to the desk.

"So far, so good. It's still too early to tell," Karen said with a smile. "What's up with you, Sergeant?"

"We may be moving you over to medical to help out the trainee. She has never worked there before, and I personally don't think she can handle it by herself."

"So whose gonna come here?"

The sergeant pulled out her piece of paper with the roster of her workers and checked it. "I'm gonna replace you with Officer Maxwell. He's a good officer for this block."

"Okay!" Karen agreed. "What time do you want me to go?"

"Let me get him over here now so you can go over there before pill line starts," the sergeant said. "Area 4 to Officer Maxwell." He responded immediately.

"3259!"

When he called the extension back, Sargent Oswald explained everything to him and told him to come over to Mike 1. About five minutes later they changed equipment, and Karen went over to medical to help the trainee out. She was already looking lost when she arrived.

"Are you okay, girl?" Karen asked, seeing how confused she looked.

"Just trying to figure out when these people are going to be ready for me to call meds," the officer said, looking at her watch.

"If they're not ready in ten minutes, just call it. We're not waiting all day for them to get ready," Karen told her, also checking the time.

It was now 3:06 p.m. Karen walked down to the nurses' station to see if they were ready for insulin. She spoke to Howard and Ingles, who were sitting at the table with Brawny. Amanda had just come out to get him so she could change his pull-up. Kayley was the infirmary nurse today. She was making a bad name for herself because she thought that she ran the place. Instead of her acting like the temp nurse that she was, she tried to be the CO, the doctor, and everything else. She was rubbing certain people the wrong way, and it wasn't just staff.

"Are you ready for insulin?" Karen asked.

"Um, yeah, you can call them now."

Karen was hoping that she said no so she could still call it anyway. She told one of the porters to close the doors to protect the patients from being exposed to anything. Everyone was taking this COVID-19 virus seriously. It had been passed down from the bosses upstairs to take drastic precautions to ensure the safety of the patients, especially Brawny. He was their priority.

During the course of running insulin, dinner had arrived. Monroe, who was in the back straightening out the linen closet, came out to help serve. He grabbed the POC trays and took them upstairs. On his way back down, he ran into his counselor. She was about to head up to talk to someone in administration about Brawny's wife that was supposed to come see him next week.

She had to make sure that all the paperwork was in before she came.

"Hey, Ms. Carmola. I was wondering if you received my request slip that had the version of my crime on it," Monroe asked as he held the door open for her.

"Yes, I've added it to your file. You'll be seeing parole in June."

Monroe was excited for the chance to hopefully finally get back home to his family and friends. Even though he messed up when he committed a crime, he hoped that everyone would see how much he'd changed and that he was ready to make a difference in society. He had been waiting for this opportunity for over two years, and now that time would be here in a couple of months.

"Thank you!"

"Tell Officer Jankoski that I'll be down to see her when I'm finished."

"Okay, I will," Monroe replied, heading back to finish helping pass out trays. He wished that Anna worked today so he could tell her the news, but she was off for two days.

~ ~ ~

Taylor finally received the call she'd been dreading. The caller told her to come to an old gas station located on Pittston Avenue at midnight. She told Steve that she was going to the market with Ashley, so he didn't suspect nothing. He was happy that she finally hung out with people other than her family, so he was oblivious to anything she was doing.

The amount of money went from five, to ten grand. She was to come alone with the money in a clear zip-lock bag and leave it in the trashcan sitting by the door. The caller also reminded her that if she told anyone, especially the cops, the video would be on the internet for all to see.

She told Ashley about the meet, and she told Karen, who had just gotten off work. She didn't even change out of her uniform. Karen didn't want Taylor going alone, so she and Ashley sat across the street from the gas station. Their car had tint on the windows so no one could see them sitting inside.

Taylor got out of the car carrying the plastic bag and walked toward the trashcan. She placed the bag inside, looking around to make sure no one snuck up on her. She heard footsteps and spun around.

"Sorry, did I scare you?" a man wearing a baseball cap asked.

By this time, Karen had already exited her vehicle with her gun by her side and eased her way over toward the gas station, making sure she wasn't seen by the man. She wanted to be close to Taylor just in case the drop didn't go as planned. Ashley kept the car running in the event they had to make a swift getaway.

"Who are you?" Taylor asked with a nervous look on her face. Out the corner of her eye, she could see Karen waiting by a parked car.

"Is it all there?" the man replied with a question of his own. He felt like he was in full control of the situation, but surely it was the other way around. Taylor nodded her head yes. He stuck his hand inside the trashcan and pulled out the zip-lock bag containing the money, the whole time keeping his eye on Taylor.

"Where is the flash drive?" The man reached into his pants pocket and pulled out his phone. He began to walk toward the same car that Karen was hiding behind. "Where is it? You said when I bring the money, you would give it to me."

"You're so naïve. See, I knew you would bring the money, so I still set up this little program just in case," he said, holding up his cellphone. "All I have to do is press Send, and your little video will be online for all to see, and I still get what I want."

"Please don't do this, you will ruin my life."

"You think this was all me? I'm not the only one behind this. You made a real enemy that wants to destroy you. However, I will tell you who it is, since I got what I wanted out of the deal. Then you can take it up with them."

Before he had the chance to say the name, there was a flash and a muffled sound. He fell forward, hitting the concrete with a loud thump. Taylor looked up in shock at Karen, who was holding the smoking gun in her hand. She rushed over and grabbed the cell phone then checked his pockets, pulling out a flash drive that was attached to a set of keys.

"Are you okay?"

"You just killed a man," Taylor said, still in shock.

"He was going to still blackmail you. I had no choice in the matter," Karen replied, looking around to make sure no one had seen what just took place. "Come on, we have to get out of here."

Taylor tried to move, but her feet stayed flat. Karen had to help her to the car. As soon as both women were in, Ashley pulled off slowly trying not to attract any attention.

"What the hell just happened?" Ashley asked.

"He was going to try to burn her. I had to do it," Karen stated, wiping the gun down with a cloth that was in the center console. She then wrapped it inside the same cloth. "We have to get rid of this gun."

Taylor sat in the back seat thinking about what just happened. A man had just been murdered in front of her. A man that was blackmailing her. What if they left some evidence that would lead the cops to them? What if someone had seen them? What if this? What if that? There were so many what-ifs running through her brain, it was driving her crazy. She was scared to death.

"As long as we stick together, no one will ever find out," Karen said as they pulled into Taylor's driveway. "I have to go take care of this weapon, so I'll see you tomorrow."

Taylor got out of the car and headed inside the house. As soon as she closed the door, the lights popped on scaring the shit out of her.

"Oh my God, you scared me," she said to Steve, who was sitting on the couch. He had this angry look on his face. "What's wrong with you?"

"Nothing," he replied, then headed in the bedroom without saying another word.

Taylor stood there with a puzzled look on her face. If anything, she should be the one with an attitude. Right now wasn't the time to worry about him. She needed to get some sleep and deal with his problem tomorrow.

FIFTEEN

It was dark when Keri turned toward the
Dunmore/Troop exit. She buzzed up the hardtop
as she pulled the Mercedes convertible off 81 onto
O'Neill Highway. Traffic was practically empty as
she pulled into the parking lot of the motel on the
right side. She walked past the front desk and
headed up one flight of stairs to room 204. Keri
tapped lightly on the door and waited. When the
door opened, Mike stood to the side, inviting her
in.

Keri had asked Carla to trade days with her at
work so she could keep her rendezvous with one
of the officers she'd been talking to. He wasn't any
ordinary officer, though. He was a lieutenant.
They would sneak around the prison whenever
plausible and get it in real quick. Tonight, though,
was different. They had invited a coworker to join
them.

Kayley was sitting in a chair next to the bed

sipping on a drink in one hand, rubbing her breasts with the other. She was high off of Molly and weed and feeling good. Keri sat on the edge of the bed as Mike poured her a drink. He opened up a capsule and poured the contents into the glass.

"This will help you relax. It's only Molly," he said, passing her the drink.

"Thank you! I see y'all got started without me."

Keri already knew what the drug was. In fact, she was the one who suggested it because it was a sexual stimulant. She took a few sips of the liquor, and before she knew it, she found herself lying on the bed in the middle of the room. Her dress and panties were on the floor. Kayley appeared above her, nude, straddling her on her hands and knees. Keri reached for her, cupping her soft, pointed breasts with hard, dark nipples. Even though they were small, they were beautiful.

Mike walked around the bed, still fully clothed. He watched as Kayley bent down and kissed Keri's breasts, suckling her nipples until they stood almost painfully erect.

"That feels good," Keri moaned.

She arched her back in ecstasy and wrapped her legs around Kayley. She was so wet that she thought a flood would pour out of her body at any second. Kayley moved lower, kissing Keri's belly. She squirmed and moaned on the bed. The inferno raging between her legs could only be extinguished by Kayley's tongue.

She ran her tongue lightly over her pussy, from bottom to top. Keri shivered and arched her back again. It wouldn't take much more to make her cum. She could feel it building already, dancing on the cusp. Mike appeared behind Kayley. He removed his shirt and let it drop to the floor. Keri couldn't take her eyes off the medallion tattoo over his chest. He must have gotten it while in the military.

"Ahhhhh," Keri continued to moan as Kayley ate her pussy like it was the last meal on earth. Keri ran her fingers through Kayley's curly hair. "Oh God, don't stop."

Mike bent down to remove his shoes. Keri

watched the well-defined muscles move under the skin of his torso. She wanted him inside her so badly. Kayley's lips on her clit made her gasp. Mike hooked his thumbs inside his pants and pushed them down. He wasn't wearing anything underneath. He stepped toward the bed, his dick growing bigger, stiffer as he approached.

Keri looked at Kayley between her legs again, but her vision blurred, and for a moment she didn't see her, only what looked like a body caressing her clean shaved pussy. She closed her eyes, letting the feel of her tongue take her to the very edge of a climax. And then she stopped.

Panting for breath, Keri opened her eyes again. Kayley crawled up the bed to lie down beside her. She kissed her, her mouth flavored with the vinegar tang of Keri's pussy, and her fingertips played lightly over her nipples.

"That is so fucking sexy," Mike whispered, looking at the two of them. "Wait till I tell them about this."

"What you say?" Keri said with a puzzled look

on her face.

"Nothing!" he replied, hoping that they didn't hear what he just said.

He grabbed Keri by her ankles and pulled her down until her ass was at the bottom edge of the bed. Kayley turned, kissing her upside down. Keri started cumming the moment Mike slid his dick inside her, wave after crashing wave of intense orgasms. She thrashed on the bed, making noises she never made before, as he slowly pulled out, almost to the point of exit, then slammed it back in. Every time he did, she shuddered with a new climax.

"Oh shiiiittt, that feels sooooo good," Keri softly moaned.

Kayley crawled on top of Keri, still upside down, spreading her thighs over her face. Between Mike's slow and steady thrusts and Kayley's tongue on her clit once again, she came so hard she thought she might pass out. Little white dots exploded behind her eyelids. She wrapped her hands around the smooth skin of

Kayley's ass and eagerly pulled her pussy down to her mouth.

She didn't make a sound, only grinding her hips above Keri's head, and continued licking her pussy. Kayley shuddered hard, pushing her pussy right up against her face as she came.

"Ahhhhghh! Fuuuck yesss!"

Now, finally, a sound escaped her throat as the orgasm steamrolled through her, a low, guttural cry that echoed off the walls like a roar. Hearing her cum made Keri so hot she thought her skin would burst into flames. Kayley lifted one leg and swung herself off of Keri. Mike pulled out, his dick dripping wet. Keri moaned in disappointment, but Kayley silenced her with a deep kiss, their tongues dancing around each other's like frisky cubs.

Mike grabbed hold of each of Keri's legs and pushed them up until her knees were against her chest. Then, effortlessly, he thrust his dick into her ass. Keri did a lot in her college days, girl on girl, two guys at once, crazy orgies, you name it, but the one thing she never did was anal. It had always been off-limits, even when she had been exclusive.

Right now, though, Keri was so horny and turned on, so willing to do anything he wanted, that she didn't care. It didn't hurt like she thought it would either. His dick slid right in on the natural lubricant from her sopping pussy. It was the most incredible feeling. Kayley kept kissing her, working her clit with her finger until she was on the brink of another orgasm. Then she stuck her finger inside Keri's pussy, and she came harder than she had all night.

Mike's breath was caught in his throat. He tilted his head back, his mouth hanging open. Keri felt his dick stiffen in her ass, then pull out. He climbed onto the bed, holding it in one hand, and positioned himself on his knees above Kayley and Keri. The first hot spurt of semen hit Keri's face, cooling immediately as it rolled down her chin. Kayley opened her mouth to receive the second, and Keri did the same.

"Damn, that was great," Mike mumbled.

A few moments later, his dick drooped, spent, and their lips, chins, and cheeks were coated in a thick white gooey liquid. Kayley kissed Keri once more, her mouth slippery and salty. Keri looked up at Mike's sweating chest. She stretched out on the bed, a satisfied hum buzzing through her body. She'd almost forgotten what it felt like to be fucked so good. Her eyelids began to close, but before they were completely closed, Keri could see Mike moving from her over to Kayley. She began stroking his dick back to life. That was all she remembered before dozing off to sleep.

~ ~ ~

The next morning when Keri woke up, she turned over to see Mike and Kayley cuddled up, spooning each other on the other side of the bed. She felt some kind of way about that. She got up and went to take a shower so she could get home. By the time she was done, they were both up and dressed, ready to go.

"Y'all nasty asses ain't going to wash up first?"

"I'll do it when I get home," Mike replied, grabbing for the doorknob.

"Me too," Kayley chimed in.

Keri gave them a blank stare and headed out the door. Mike got in his truck and pulled off without saying bye to the women. As Kayley was about to get in her car, Keri stopped her, with a suspicious look on her face.

"Hey!" Kayley turned to her. "How long was you two there before I got there?"

"Not long, why?"

"Nothing, just wanted to know. I'll see you at work later," Keri said, getting in the car.

The whole drive home Keri thought about what they did last night and if it was a mistake. Everyone had told her that Kayley was easy, but she didn't know it would be that easy. She decided to see how far she was willing to go. She called her friend who was a sergeant at the prison.

"Hey, I have a job for you!"

SIXTEEN

Tara sat in her office, preparing her staffing packets for all the inmates that were coming up for parole within the next four months. Amongst those packets were Monroe's. She liked him because he was a good worker and stayed off the radar. Whenever she or the unit manager needed help with something and they had to use an inmate's assistance, they would call him. That was one of the reasons she was going to make sure he got the institution's approval for parole.

As she was typing on her computer, she received a call from the block officer, letting her know the inmate that she called was here. Dread walked into her office with a smile on his face.

"Good morning, Ms. Carmola," he said, taking a seat in the chair.

"Good morning," Tara replied. "Why are you smiling? You must know that I have some good news for you."

"My name was on the callout to sign my paperwork today. I'm just waiting for property to call and tell me to pack my stuff."

"Oh good. So I didn't have to call you down because you already knew, then. Would you like to call someone and see if they can pick you up tomorrow, or are you taking public transport-ation?"

Dread called his girl and gave her the good news. Tamika wasn't really his girl. She was someone he met while in prison who had been riding his bid out. He ended up using her for money and other things when he found out that she was a big girl. Dread loved his women with some meat on them, but she was obese. She came to visit him one day and could hardly fit in the chair. At that point, he decided to use her for whatever he could get.

After telling her what time to pick him up, he ended the call. Tara checked some other things out for him before he had to leave.

"I told you I would do whatever I could to get

you out, didn't I?" she said with a smile.

"Yes you did. Thank you so much."

"Take care of yourself, and don't come back," Tara said, signing his pass.

"I won't, trust me," Dread replied, heading out of her office.

As soon as he was gone, Tara headed over to her other office on K block. As she walked through the infirmary, she ran into Renata. She was working a double shift today because one of the nurses had to be escorted out this morning. She was showing possible signs for the COVID-19 virus. As a precaution, they had to get her out of there before she spread it throughout the prison. That would have been a catastrophe.

"Hey, what's up?" Renata said when Tara walked past.

"Hey!"

Tara spoke even though she really didn't like the workers on second shift. To her, it seemed like they were too full of themselves. They walked around like they ran the place, and that didn't sit right with her. When she got to K block, Karen was sitting at the desk talking to another officer. From the looks of it, whatever they were talking about was serious. As she approached, the conversation suddenly stopped.

"Don't stop talking now," she said sarcastically.

They both laughed, then continued talking about something totally different until she left. Once she was out of earshot, Karen continued their original conversation.

"If you want to be a part of our group, you will have to prove yourself. I'm the dominant one, so what do you consider yourself as?" Karen asked.

"I have always considered myself as a butch. I tried to be a fem before, but that wasn't working. I had to be the dominant one, so I guess you can say that I'm the butch," Officer Barnes stated.

Anita Barnes was still a trainee. She had about three months left before becoming a permanent correctional officer. She had proven numerous times that she could handle herself in many situations. Karen was looking for another person like herself to help recruit some more women for their group. She didn't want to be the only butch there.

"So we will be planning something soon, will you be free to attend?"

"Just let me know when it is and I will move some things around to be there," Anita replied.

Officer Barnes received a call over the radio, causing her to leave in a hurry. As soon as she was gone, Karen made her rounds and checked on all the inmates.

~ ~ ~

"I really don't see why you stay with him," Stone said, drinking a glass of wine.

He and Gina were sitting in the living room watching the news. President Trump was talking about the plans they put in motion to try to help the nation get through this epidemic virus. It had already claimed over a hundred lives and was only going to get worse before it got better. They had created over a million tests.

"Because he is the father of my child," Gina snapped, taking a swig of her own drink. Her glass was almost empty, so she filled it back up.

Truth be told, she was starting to wonder the same thing. Gina had a feeling he was lying about ending his relationship with his wife, so she hired a private investigator to look into it. When he left the other day to go back home, she had checked his Instagram account and found a recent post of him and his family out at an arcade somewhere in Scranton.

Gina knew it was recent because of the background. On a clock on the wall, the date was the same day he left. Until the PI got back to her with some hard evidence, she was inclined to believe that maybe he was just out because of their daughter.

"I know you so-called love this guy, but you need to start facing the truth, Sis. He's never gonna leave her for you."

"Shut up! You don't know what you're talking about," she yelled. She downed her drink, then poured another. There was something on her mind that she wanted to get out. "And since you're always in my business I think you should know that we're not really related."

"Sit your ass down somewhere. You're just drunk and talking out the side of your neck," Stone replied, pouring more wine into his glass. "If anything, your dumb ass is the one adopted."

"I'm serious. You were adopted when you were a baby. Mom and Dad never told you, but I knew."

"How?" Stone asked, wondering if what she was saying had any truth to it.

"I was going through some of their stuff and found this," she said, walking over to the drawer, pulling out a manilla envelope and passing it to Stone. "Everything you need to know is inside there."

When Stone read all the contents of the envelope, he couldn't believe his eyes. It was there clear as day that he had been adopted when he was born. It said that his real mother was a drug addict, and the father was killed in a drug bust. He looked up at his sister, who by now was sitting on the arm of the chair. She felt bad for telling him the truth like that, but at the same time she felt like he should know.

"How long have you known about this?"

"Not long! Like I said, I was going through some of their stuff and stumbled across it. I wasn't looking for anything. I was just going to throw some stuff out. Stone, I'm sorry that I said it like that. You will always be my brother," Gina stated, giving him a hug.

The wine wasn't doing anything for them anymore, so Gina pulled out the hard liquor. They sat in the living room getting so drunk that they both passed out on the couch.

~ ~ ~

Gina woke up around ten o'clock that night with her head in Stone's lap. She was still feeling tipsy from all the drinking they were doing earlier. When she sat up, she noticed that her brother had a hard-on. Staring at it made her horny. Without even realizing what she was doing, Gina's hand reached over and rubbed the bulge in his pants. When Stone didn't move, she stuck her hand down his pants.

Even though her plan was to marry Steve, ever since she had found out that Stone wasn't her real brother, she had fantasized about doing things with him. The liquor was enhancing those emotions, causing her to do things that a sober mind wouldn't even consider. She slowly removed it from its captivity, and it stood at attention. It wasn't as big as Steve's, but it had potential.

She placed the tip in her mouth, letting her tongue twirl around the opening. Stone still hadn't moved an inch yet. The only thing that seemed to be functioning at the moment was his dick, which was the only thing she needed to be working right now. Gina began to deep-throat him, taking all seven inches in her mouth. Her head bounced up and down.

The slurping sounds got louder and louder,

then she stopped and stood up in front of him. She unfastened the jeans she was wearing and pulled them off, leaving on her white silk panties. When she removed her shirt, her firm breasts snuck out of her bra. She got down on her knees and continued sucking his dick, at the same time, placing a hand between her legs fingering her own pussy. She could feel his dick start to jerk in her mouth.

Gina stood up and straddled his lap. She pulled her panties to the side and sat on his dick. She started rotating her hips from side to side, then up and down. The feeling of an orgasm was quickly building inside of her, causing her to move faster. Suddenly his eyes popped open a little. Gina was so busy trying to cum, that she never noticed. Stone gripped her ass cheeks.

"Is this what you want?" he whispered, lifting her body up without letting the tip come out, then bringing it back down with force.

"Oh my God, baby, yesss. That feels so good," Gina moaned, wrapping her arms around his neck tightly.

Her body started shivering out of control, and her eyes rolled into the back of her head. Soon as she came, Stone followed right behind her with a thunderous orgasm of his own.

"Damn," Stone said. Then reality kicked in. He was no longer drunk, looking at Gina. "What the hell did we just do?"

She didn't have an answer for him. His dick was still lodged inside her, shrinking by the second. Finally, he lifted her off his lap and fixed his clothes.

"I'm sorry. We were both drunk, and I thought you were someone else," Gina lied. Truth was, she was so desperate to have another baby that she didn't care how she got it. If it worked, she was going to lie to Steve and say that it was his.

"This shouldn't have happened, and it won't happen again. You're my fucking sister for Christ's sake."

"I'm not your real sister, and don't act like you haven't been thinking about doing this. I have seen the way you watch me when I get out of the shower, or when I walk around in my bikini."

"You are out of your fucking mind, Gina. You need some help," Stone said, shaking his head. "Was that why you told me about the whole adoption in the first place?"

"I told you because I thought you should know. I wish I'd never found that damn envelope," Gina complained as she grabbed her own clothes and ran to her room.

Stone sat on the couch thinking about what they just did. It was at that moment that he realized that there was a possibility that he did have intimate feelings for his own sister, even if they weren't blood relatives. He used to get mad whenever she brought a man home, and he did use to watch her a bit too much when she walked around the house wearing hardly anything. Now that he found out that she wasn't his sister and they just had sex, would that change their lives forever?

SEVENTEEN

Taylor woke up in a cold sweat. She had been having nightmare after nightmare the last couple of days, and it wasn't getting any better. Every time she heard anything that resembled a gunshot, she would jump out of her skin. She could still see the man's body dropping to the ground, blood spilling out the color of crimson, and the look on Karen's face like she had done that before. That scared her the most because she didn't know who she was really living next to. Tears escaped her eyes as she sat there with her blanket pulled up to her shoulders.

Her husband had been giving her the cold shoulder ever since she came home late that night, and their daughter wondered what was going on between them. He turned over briefly, looked at her, then turned back the other way like he didn't care. Taylor knew her marriage was coming to an end, but there was still a part of her that wouldn't believe it.

She got out of bed and went to the kitchen. After turning on the coffee pot, she took out a couple of English muffins and tossed them in the toaster. Once she spread the butter and jelly on them and poured a cup of coffee, she sat down at the kitchen table and watched CNN. All they continued to talk about was the COVID-19 virus and how it had expanded throughout the United States. She finished off her muffin and coffee, then decided to head back to bed.

Steve was up now, texting someone on his phone. Taylor didn't say anything to him. She got back in bed and tried to go back to sleep.

"So are you ready to talk about the other night?" Steve asked, sitting his phone on the nightstand.

Taylor sat up. "What is there to talk about? You think I was out with someone other than Karen and Ashley, but you won't go ask them yourself."

"Because I shouldn't have to. I asked my wife

a simple question. Are you messing around, and you refuse to answer."

"You know I would never cheat on you," she lied, still thinking about the orgy she had with her newfound friends. Just the thought of how Ashley ate her pussy made her moist.

"Do I?" he replied. "I'm on a damn boat for months. How do I know what you're doing while I'm gone?"

"Oh, so you just gonna sit there and accused me of having an affair? You got some fucking nerve," Taylor snapped back, finally getting the strength to confront her husband. "I do know something about you though."

He had just opened the door of no return, and Taylor decided that it was time to show her hand. She hopped out of bed, walked over to her drawer, pulled out the envelope containing photos of Steve and his other family, and threw it at him. When he opened up the envelope discovering all the photos, his face turned a different color. He had to take a second look to be sure.

"Where did you get these from?" Taylor didn't reply. He got louder. "I said where did you get these from?"

"Fuck all that. How do you have a whole other family, and you acting like I'm the one doing something wrong?" Taylor said, standing there with her hands on her hips, anger evident in her voice.

All his anger suddenly subsided. There was nothing Steve could say or do, except admit to his own guilt. He was caught red-handed. All the commotion had awakened their daughter. She knocked on the door.

"Mommy, Daddy, are you okay?"

Taylor hurried over to the door and opened it. Trinity was standing there with a worried look on her face, wiping her eyes.

"Yes, baby, we're just discussing something. Sorry if we were too loud," smiled Taylor. "Go back to bed, and I'll be in there in a few minutes to tuck you in."

"I'm not a kid anymore, Mommy. I can tuck myself in. I just wanted to make sure you and Daddy were okay."

"You're right, baby. Go back to bed and let us finish talking, okay?" Taylor could only admire her daughter's wittiness.

Once she was gone, they continued with their argument until Steve got dressed and left. Even with this virus spreading and the governor shutting the state down, he still decided to leave. Taylor was livid that he just ran out like that instead of staying and finishing their conversation. She began blowing his phone up, to only keep getting his voicemail. That's when she started sending him obscene messages. As soon as she sent the sixth message, there was a knock at the door. Thinking it was him, she swung it open hard as hell.

"Why the fuck you just leav—"

Taylor stopped in midsentence because it wasn't Steve. It was Ashley standing there with her mouth wide open.

"I just came over to see if everything was okay," she said nervously. She had never seen Taylor this mad before. "Did I come at a bad time?"

"No, come in," Taylor said, stepping to the side to let her in. "Me and my husband just had a terrible argument and he left. Can I get you something to drink?"

"No, I'm good! Are you okay?" Ashley asked, leaning against the wall. She was wearing a pair of white see-through tights that left nothing to the imagination, and a burgundy sweater. Her hair was up in a bun, and she had no makeup on, showing that she was still beautiful without it.

"If you're talking about him, yes, I'm good, but if you're talking about what happened the other night, then hell no. This shit has been haunting me. Why didn't she just scare him or something?"

Taylor stood there lost in her own thoughts. Ashley could see that she was really shaken up by what Karen did. She walked over to where she stood and ran a finger through her hair.

"Baby, he was going to hurt you, and Karen would never let that happen." Ashley's hand ran down her face. It was soft and warm. "Why don't you come over to our house and we can all talk about it?"

"I can't, my daughter is here," Taylor replied, moving away from her and looking at Trinity's room.

"What about tonight?"

"I don't think I'll be able to," Taylor said. "Matter of fact, I think that me joining y'all's group was a mistake. I was lonely at the time and let my guard down."

"Are you sure that's how you feel," Ashley asked, invading her private space. She was so close that she could feel the heat radiating off Taylor's body. She stuck her hand under her shirt, lifting her bra over her perky breasts. Ashley squeezed one of her nipples while whispering in her ear. "Are you really sure that I can't persuade you to change your mind?"

Taylor's pussy was tingling from the fire that

Ashley had started, but she was able to hold her ground. She eased out of her space. Her titties were still out of her bra.

"Yes, I'm sure. I have to go check on my daughter," she said, walking over to the door. She opened it up, giving Ashley the hint that it was time to go. "If I need anything, I'll surely give you a call."

"Okay," Ashley said, walking out the door. As she walked by, her fingers purposely felt Taylor's pussy. Ashley smiled.

Taylor shut the door and leaned up against it. She slid her breasts back inside her bra and sighed because Ashley had left her pussy wet as fuck and she needed some dick bad. She wished that she and Steve and hadn't argued earlier. She could sure use his dick inside her pussy right now. Instead, she had to settle for a cold shower. Trinity came out of her room holding the phone in her hand.

"Mommy, can I go over to Jenny's house and play for a while? Please, Mommy, please?"

"Oh, so now you want to play the baby act, huh?" Taylor joked. "I thought you weren't a baby anymore."

Trinity gave her mother a big hug hoping that she would say yes. Knowing that she needed to release some stress, Taylor decided to let her go.

"Thank you, Mommy. I'm on my way there," Trinity told her friend before ending the call.

"Do not leave from over there until I come get you," Taylor firmly stated. "Understand?"

"Yes, Mommy," Trinity replied.

Taylor walked her daughter over to her friend's house, which was only down the block, and then came back home. Since the stores were about to close because of the state of emergency that was issued, she decided to pick up some milk, bread and eggs. She needed to hurry up and get back home because her pussy was still tingling. As she paid for her groceries and was heading out the door, a silver F150 with tinted windows pulled up in front of her. It scared her. The passenger-side window rolled down.

"So we meet again," the driver said.

"Why are you down this way?" Taylor asked, trying to hide the fact that she was a bit excited to see him.

"I don't know. Maybe I want you to get in so we can talk," Boris replied.

"Why don't you get out and we can talk right here?"

"Okay, but if your husband rides past and see us, what will he think?"

Taylor thought about that for a minute, then realized that he was right. It would only fuel his suspicions if he saw her talking to another man. She looked around to see if anyone was watching before stepping inside his truck. She placed her two bags on the floor in front of her.

"You can give me a ride to the corner of my block."

Boris was wearing a wifebeater, with his biceps out. She had to cross her legs to stop her juices from leaking out and soaking her panties. He noticed what she was doing right away, and decided to egg her on a bit. He reached over between her legs and palmed her pussy. At first she tried to play like she didn't want him to do that, until his finger kept tapping her clit. It started feeling good, causing her to open up her legs, giving him more access.

"I see someone is starting to like it. You wanna go somewhere private real quick and have some fun?" She didn't respond at first. He stuck his hand down her pants to see how wet she was. "Damn, girl, it feels like you peed on yourself. Does that mean your answer is yes?"

"We can't go far because my daughter is over at her friend's house playing," Taylor replied, grabbing his hand and pushing it inside her.

She was so horny now that if she didn't get the dick from him, she might fuck the first nigga she saw. That would have been a bad idea. Boris pulled into a parking lot near the trails and parked out of eyesight of passing traffic. A soon as he put the car in park, Taylor had his dick out of his pants and in her mouth. She was sucking it like it was the last dick on earth. Boris hit the button, pulling his seat all the way back.

That was Taylor's cue. She pulled one leg out of her pants and hopped on his lap. His dick slid in easily as she tongued him down. They fucked for a good ten minutes before cumming in unison. Boris dropped Taylor off at the corner of her block, then headed home.

Taylor felt like she wasn't fully satisfied, but it would have to do for now. Once again she started to feel bad for her actions. It was a forbidden passion that she just couldn't hide. She showered and took a nap before she had to pick Trinity up.

EIGHTEEN

Shit hit the fan inside of the prison. A couple of staff members tested positive for the coronavirus, causing the superintendent to put the whole institution on lockdown. They didn't know how many inmates the infected staff members came in contact with, so they needed to take all precautions to isolate it. They moved all the inmates off one unit and turned it into a quarantine unit.

Monroe and three other inmates were asked to move into the infirmary to take care of the patients. They set up four beds in the dayroom so they could live. The only good thing that came from it was he got to see his favorite nurse whenever she was there. She had told him that she was going to work a double, so she would be there all night. That was like music to his ears.

"I got the nightshift tonight," Monroe told his coworkers as they sat there playing cards.

It was around nine thirty at night and everything was quiet in the infirmary. Since everything was locked down, there was no inmate movement. The only people walking around was staff.

"Good, 'cause I'm trying to get some sleep and you know Brawny is probably going to be up around one or two in the morning," Tony said as they finished up their game and were now settling down for the night.

"I got him." Monroe wasn't too worried about Brawny because he had already told Anna to give him an extra shot of his sleeping medicine so he would be good for the rest of the night.

Around ten, third shift was starting to pour in. Paula and Irene spoke to the inmate porters as they headed to the nurses' station. Paula looked at Monroe in a way that she never had looked at him before. She would usually speak and keep it moving, but tonight she gave him an awkward stare. Not thinking anything of it, he headed to the back isolation room where they had moved

Brawny. He was already sleeping.

Anna walked in and told him that she had to make some rounds and that she should be back in about an hour. Monroe nodded his head and watched as she walked out. She had on her gray scrubs tonight that showed how fat her pussy was. He couldn't wait to at least get to feel it, even if he couldn't get any tonight because of how much staff was walking around.

Since Brawny was sleep, Monroe came out to fill up his pitcher with ice and water. Officer Jankoski was working the overnight shift also. Monroe walked over to where she was sitting.

"Damn, they got you working overnight also?"

"Yep, it's safer in here than it is out there," she joked. "Shit, I need that thirty dollars an hour. I'm trying to go to the Bahamas this summer."

"You better hope that it's safe to travel by then," Monroe stated.

They talked for a few more minutes, and then he walked back down to the isolation room. As he passed the nurses station, Paula once again gave him this awkward look. He wanted to say something but didn't. He sat down in the reclining chair and watched television. He flipped through the channels until he found something that he wanted to watch on Bravo. *Blind Date* was on. He was hoping that Anna would hurry up and come back because he was bored and needed something to do. He waited so long that he ended up falling asleep.

~ ~ ~

Monroe woke up to a feeling all too familiar to him. A warm mouth had his dick at full attention. Anna had finally come to see him. The feeling of her mouth had him ready to shoot his load.

"Oh shit, you finally was able to come see me," he moaned, opening his eyes.

When he was able to focus, it wasn't Anna that was performing oral on him, it was Paula. This took Monroe by total surprise. He never saw this coming at all. Maybe this was the reason she kept staring at him when he walked by. At the moment he didn't care.

"Anna told me that you had a big dick, but damn," she said, coming up for air. She stroked his dick while staring him in the eyes. "This is bigger than I've ever seen."

"Oh really?" Monroe mumbled, trying to push her head back down on his dick. She got the hint and continued her business.

Paula had been working the nightshift for quite some time now. She was forty-two years old, skinny, and wasn't bad looking at all. What left a memorable impression on Monroe was her walk. She was bowlegged, and every time she walked, it made her look even sexier. Now she was down on her knees giving him a blow job. Then he thought about Anna and her coming in and catching them. He gently pushed Paula's head away.

"What's wrong?" she asked.

"Nothing's wrong. We just can't be doing this," Monroe replied, looking over to the window. The shades on the outside were pulled down, giving them privacy.

"If you're worried about getting caught, don't.

Karen knows what we are doing and will let us know if we get some unwanted company." She smiled. "If you're worried about Anna, she is too busy over on C2, taking care of a patient that fell out of bed. She won't be back for a while. Just relax and let me take care of you."

"Why do you want to do this?" Monroe questioned.

"I told you why already. Anna was bragging about how big your dick was and how you always left her walking bowlegged after y'all had sex. I wanted to see if it was true. I won't tell if you don't."

Monroe was lost for words. That quickly changed when Paula stood up in front of him and untied the drawstring on her scrubs. When she let them fall to the floor, she stood there in a pair of white panties. They were tight and showed her pussy print, but nothing like the ones that Anna wore. He felt like he was cheating on her, and was trying to make up his mind if he should or shouldn't. When she pulled off her panties,

Monroe eyes were mesmerized at how beautiful her pussy looked.

"You're beautiful!"

"Thank you," Paula replied. "I don't think we have all night, so if you want to get in this, you better come on before it's too late."

She looked at Brawny, then sat on the edge of the bed, spreading her legs open. Monroe jumped out of his chair fast. He got down on his knees and tried to eat her pussy, but she stopped him.

"You can do that some other time. Right now, I just want to see how your dick feels. If I start screaming, just cover my mouth, but don't stop. I have to see how deep you can go."

Monroe positioned himself in front of her and stuck the tip of his dick inside her. She squirmed a little but wanted more. By the time he was halfway in, she couldn't take it anymore. She tried to push him back, but Monroe was persistent. He could tell that whoever she had been fucking previously had a little dick. Her pussy was wet, but it also was super tight. He covered her mouth with his, sticking his tongue inside connecting with hers, and pushed more of his dick inside her tight hole.

"How does it feel now?" he whispered.

"Mmmmmm," she moaned. That was the only words she could get out. By now it was beginning to feel good. Her body was trying to move in rhythm with his.

That was the only problem Monroe had when it came to sex. He liked making love to his women instead of just fucking them. There was a good consequence to it all. Most of the women he laid pipe to would fall in love with his dick game and keep coming back for more.

"Damn, you feel so fucking good," Monroe whispered in her ear. He was now deep inside her. She was taking all ten inches. "This how you like it?"

"Yesss, baby, fuck this pussy," Paula screamed. Every thrust he gave her, she would scream out in ecstasy and pain.

At that moment Monroe couldn't contain

himself. He gave her exactly what she wanted. Her legs were now in a spread-eagle position, and even though it was dark, he could still see her pussy glistening.

"I'm about to cum," Monroe moaned, leaning down and sucking on one of her titties.

"Me too! Just don't cum in me," she replied, knowing how fertile she was.

Monroe took a couple more pumps and tried to pull out, shooting his sperm all over her stomach. It was so good that he didn't want to at first. Some still got inside her. Paula took a towel and wiped herself clean, then pulled up her clothes.

"I can't believe he slept through all that," she said, looking at Brawny.

"That's because he took his meds late tonight. He should be cool until tomorrow morning."

"I'm gonna need some more of this," she said, grabbing his dick. "Can we keep this a secret from Anna?"

"As long as you don't run your mouth to

anyone, I'm straight with it," Monroe replied, then pulled her into his body and kissed her like she had never been kissed before. "I can tell that your husband ain't fucking you right. You need that pussy tamed, and I'm just the one to do it."

"Is that right?"

"Ask Anna," he said, trying to be smart. When she looked at him funny, he stuck his finger inside her scrubs, feeling her pussy, then stuck it in her mouth. "Taste it. That's what I do to people."

Paula tasted her own juices, sucking everything off his fingers. She had to admit to herself that his big black dick had her turned out. She walked out of the room even more bowlegged than when she came in. The smile on Monroe's face was priceless. He had two women that wanted the dick. Never did he imagine that he would be getting so much pussy in prison and from two beautiful women.

He even started reconsidering the agreement he made with Anna. Did he really want to settle down with her when he was released? It was something for him to really think about before he got out in a few months. He just had to be careful, because if someone found out about it, he would immediately be transferred from that institution, and maybe even charged and sent to the hole.

NINETEEN

Naked in the dark, Karen and Ashley kicked back on their queen-size bed after their lovemaking, watching a show called *For Life*. Right before that, Karen had turned on the ten o'clock news to see if there were any new updates on that night when she shot that man trying to hurt Taylor. Other than the police saying that it was a gang-related murder, there was no new information.

"Have you even tried to talk to Taylor?" Ashley asked her wife. Karen shook her head no. "You said that you would talk to her."

"I know what I said, and I will," she replied, giving Ashley the evil eye.

"I just think that she hasn't been in her right state of mind since that night. When I tried to talk to her, she brushed me off."

Ashley left out the part that she tried to seduce Taylor again. She didn't want Karen to know that she did it behind her back. Ashley was becoming obsessed with Taylor. That night at the hotel had triggered something that she never felt before. It was like Taylor was her forbidden pleasure, and she needed to have her one way or the other.

"Since I don't have to work tomorrow, I will talk to her," Karen said, getting up to use the bathroom.

As she walked past her window, she could see Taylor standing on her porch talking to her husband. He was standing there in sweats, and his bags were on the ground beside him. Whatever they were talking about, the conversation was getting heated. Steve threw his bags in the back of his SUV and then got in the driver's seat and pulled off.

"What are you looking at?" Ashley asked.

"I think they just broke up," Karen replied. "They looked like they were arguing and he put his bags in his car and left. She just went back into the house."

"This might be the perfect time for you to go

over there and make sure she's alright."

"I'll go over in the morning when she's had time to calm down."

"Okay, but after you finish in the bathroom, you think I can get some more of that dick?"

Karen laughed. "Sure, pull it out and I'll be right back."

~ ~ ~

Kayley was sitting in the Infectious Control Office by herself because she couldn't be in the nurses' station with the other nurses. They didn't like the smell of her perfume, which was really her shampoo, because it was supposedly making them sick. The truth was, they were kind of jealous of her. She was young and the new eye candy of the prison, and they had already run their course in the other staff's eyes.

She was sitting at the desk on the computer looking up a book called *Breaking the Chains* by Ernest Morris, because she knew him personally and wanted him to autograph it for her. Sergeant Reed tapped on the door and opened it.

"What are you doing in here?"

"Apparently my shampoo is making the other staff sick, so instead of sitting in there arguing with them, I just came in here."

"You're joking, right?" Reed said.

"I wish I was. I'm starting to think that them bitches are jealous of me. I know I'm only a temp, but they don't have to treat me like that. I would never do that to them."

He could see her eyes tearing up. He stepped all the way into the office and closed the door. He felt bad that they were treating her like that. Usually he would enjoy the newbies getting hazed, but this time was different.

"Don't cry, Kayley," he said in a comforting voice. He placed his arm around her, bringing her into his body.

Kayley could feel his package swelling up on her shoulder. It didn't feel so big, but it still made her feel horny. She reached over and felt it. Reed didn't even flinch. This was what he wanted anyway. After talking to Keri the other day, this was going better than he had expected. They had made a bet that Kayley wouldn't let him fuck her.

"We can't do this here," Kayley said, moving her hand.

"I know a spot where we can go real quick if you have time," Reed stated. When she didn't respond, he stuck his hand down her sweater, feeling her breasts that were just enough to cup.

She looked at the clock. She still had about forty-five minutes before she had to be back on C2. She logged out of the computer and got up to leave.

"Where we going?"

"Come on, I'll show you."

They went down the back stairs to the basement, and into one of the examination rooms. Reed knew that no one would be coming down there, so they had all the privacy they needed. As soon as he closed the door, Kayley pushed him up against the wall and began to unhook his belt. Reed started kissing her, at the same time sticking his hand down the back of her jeans, feeling her ass. It was soft.

Once she had his pants unbuckled and unfastened, Kayley unzipped her jeans and pulled them down with her panties as quickly as she could. She stepped out of them, leaving them on the floor. Reed sat down in the chair, motioning for Kayley to come sit on his lap. She turned around and backed on top of him, sliding her pussy down on his dick. The head went in, and then she let her weight down so that his dick was unilaterally inclined to fuck.

"Oh God," she said. "You feel good inside me. This is just what I needed."

Reed wrapped both his arms around her and began to kiss her earlobes and her hair. His fingers started pulling up her sweater until he had it at her shoulders. He grabbed her titties and fondled them while she leaned back against his chest. Kayley rocked back and forth on his dick. It felt so good to her that she tried to squeeze her own breasts, but he still had a grip on them.

"Just ride it, baby," he whispered. "Your shit is

so tight and wet. I see why them bitches is jealous now."

"Yeah, that's because this pussy is the bomb, right?" she moaned, feeling her orgasm forming.

One of his hands slid down her soft bare skin and reached for her clit. Reed licked his middle finger and started circling it, causing Kayley to move her body faster.

"You sure can take a lot of dick to have such a small body."

Kayley wanted to laugh at his dick comment, but she was feeling good right now. Even though it was so small, he knew exactly what to do with it. He fiddled with her pussy until he made her cum. She was breathing hard now from how sweet his fingers felt. He kept fingering her while she rode his dick.

"I'm about to cum," he said, pulling out.

Kayley quickly got down on her knees and placed his dick in her mouth. She sucked him until all his semen went down her throat. After sucking him dry, she stood up.

"You think you have one more round in you?"

Without even answering, Reed stood up and picked Kayley up, sitting her on the examining table. He put his hand between her legs and stuck his finger into her pussy. Kayley was still all juicy and slippery from the pounding she just took. When he pulled his finger out, it was covered in her cum. He stuck it in his mouth, sucking it for a while.

"Dee-licious," he said. "This taste better than a peppermint.

He put his hands out and spread her legs apart. Then he kneeled over her, guiding his dick into the sticky place between her legs. It felt so good that he thought he would bust immediately. The deeper he went, the more her pussy muscles gripped his dick. Her insides began to melt with pleasure. Reed's pounding got faster and harder. Kayley opened her legs even more.

"Control to Area 4," his radio interrupted his strokes. As much as he didn't want to stop, he didn't want to get in trouble either. He grabbed it off his belt.

"Area 4, go 'head."

"At your convenience, 3232."

"Give me about four mikes," he replied, setting the radio back down. "We have to hurry up. I only have about three minutes and then I have to stop and call them back."

"Well you better hurry up," she moaned, closing her eyes.

He started pumping her pussy like he was about to die. She grabbed his ass cheeks, assisting him by moving his body in and out of her. It only took about twelve more pumps before he was shooting his load again, this time inside her. Kayley stood up and felt Reed's hot jism running down the inside of her leg. She walked over to one of the cabinets and pulled out a towel, wiping herself. She passed it to him so that he could wipe his dick off.

"You better call control back before they come looking for you."

"They can wait," he replied, putting his pants

back on. Kayley quickly put her clothes on also.

They headed back upstairs, and Sergeant Reed made his phone call. Some of the porters were sitting at the table playing cards when Kayley took the walk of shame down the hall past them. She could tell that they knew she just got finished doing something, but didn't know what.

After Sergeant Reed finished what he was doing, he went into the 10 to 6 room and made an outside phone call. Soon as the caller answered, he smiled.

"You owe me. That shit was too easy. I just got finish fucking the shit out of her in the spot. I'll tell you about it when I get off," he said, then ended the call. He walked out of the room and headed over to M1.

Monroe was just wiping down all the doorknobs when he heard his whole conversation. It didn't take a rocket scientist to know who the person was. He wondered if he should tell her what he just heard. She was really cool with him, and they talked about a lot of shit. They were supposed to link up for drinks when he came home in a couple of months. He kept on cleaning and decided to think long and hard before saying something.

TWENTY

"I wanted you to see this before I sent the results over to the DA's office," the ME said to the officer, pointing at something on the computer screen.

He sat down in front of the desk the ME was sitting at. She had a diagram up of the victim of what they thought was a gang-related shooting. What it showed was that this wasn't gang-related. However, it was a homicide.

"I've already sent my findings to your captain," the ME stated. "Whoever did this didn't think that anyone would look into it thoroughly. This case is still officially open."

"Well I guess I won't be getting any sleep tonight. I have to go back out to that neighborhood and interview some people."

"Where is your partner?"

"She was supposed to meet me here, but got stuck investigating a kidnapping that may be linked to a case that we were working on a few months ago."

"What is going on in our country? Not only is this COVID-19 killing people, but we still have people out there that don't want to listen and still running the streets committing crimes."

"Girl, that is the truth," Detective Myers stated. "The governor should just declare martial law and let the National Guard take over. I bet people would stay at home then until this shit is under control. If you'll excuse me for a moment while I update my boss on this new information."

The medical examiner went back to getting the rest of her corpses ready for transport to the different funeral homes. Detective Myers told her captain about the findings, and that she was going to follow up on a couple more leads before going home. As soon as she ended the call, her partner walked in looking like she had just stepped off a modeling runway.

"So where are we heading first, partner?"

"You look like you need to be on the front

cover of someone's magazine, instead of investigating homicides," Myers said.

"Oh, so you like this, huh?" she replied, spinning around so her partner could see the full outfit.

"Where the hell are you going? I thought you were supposed to be checking out a kidnapping lead."

"I did. Can't a girl look presentable when she's working?" Officer Robinson joked.

Officer Cheryl Robinson was coming up on her third year as a homicide detective. She transferred from Brooklyn, New York, about four years ago because of some personal reasons that she kept a secret. She met her partner when they were both at a charity event in Carbondale. They both requested to team up, and their captain approved it. Now they were at the top of their game, and the men hated that they had a conviction rate that was higher than any of theirs.

Maybe it had something to do with the fact that they were both drop-dead gorgeous and men and women would try to bed them. It was easy for either of them to get a confession from a suspect. All they really had to do was charm them a little, and they would have anyone eating out the palm of their hands. Cheryl was bisexual, but Diana wasn't. She tried licking pussy when she was in college, but wasn't feeling it. She promised herself that if there was one person that she would try it again with, it would be Cheryl. She had a big-time crush on her partner but never acted on it.

One time when they stayed in a hotel room together because they had to pick up a suspect out in Jersey City, Cheryl noticed Diana staring at her in the shower. Trying to be funny, she kept bending over giving her a full view of her pussy. She could see Diana getting all excited as she performed for her. Then when she would turn around, she would act like she was sleeping. Since then, she would tease her every chance she got.

"You better always look good. Don't nobody want no broke bitch that looks like they just shopped at the thrift store," Diana stated.

"Right!" The two women slapped hands and left.

They both hopped in Diana's car and headed over to where the crime took place. When they arrived, there weren't many people out walking around. They looked for any signs of a camera on or around the gas station.

"His body was here," Diana stated. "So if anyone saw anything, they would have had to been looking from over there."

She was pointing to an area across the street from where they were standing. Cheryl looked in that direction and then looked for cameras, but to no avail. The two of them knocked on doors to see if anyone saw or heard anything that night, and still came up empty-handed. Cheryl came to the assumption that whoever murdered that man had to have had some kind of suppression on their weapon.

After hours of knocking on doors and questioning passersby, Diana was ready to go home. Since she lived all the way in Wilkes-Barre, she decided to stay at Cheryl's.

"Thanks for letting me stay here tonight," Diana said, spreading a blanket over the couch.

"If you're not comfortable sleeping there, my bed is super big enough for the both of us. My door is always open if you want to come in."

"Thanks, partner."

Cheryl headed into her room, and Diana sat down on the couch and started watching television. It seemed like every channel she turned to, they were talking about that damn coronavirus. She decided to check out her Instagram account and see what was new. Even they were talking about how the Simpsons had predicted all of this before it happened. Fed up with all the talk, she set her phone down and tried to get some rest.

Cheryl woke up to a moaning sound. She looked around the room but didn't see anyone. Sitting up on her bed, she waited until her eyes were fully focused before getting up. As she walked toward the door, the moaning got louder.

The first thing she thought was that Diana had invited some man over and they were having sex on her couch. When she looked out the door, Diana was lying on the couch naked.

Cheryl was expecting to see a man between her legs eating her pussy, but instead, all she saw was Diana's fingers performing oral pleasure. She stood there for a minute watching her. She had her eyes closed, and one leg was on the back of the couch. She had two fingers deep inside her pussy.

Cheryl eased her way over to Diana, crawling on all fours until she was right in front of her. The sight of her pussy lips had her mouthwatering. Cheryl could smell the aroma coming from her opening. She bent down so close to her that her tongue was inches away. Before Diana knew what was happening, Cheryl licked her clit twice. Her eyes popped open.

"Cheryl, what are you doing?" she asked in a stunned voice.

"I thought you could use some assistance," Cheryl replied with a smile on her face. Diana started blushing, but didn't cover herself up.

"Well, since you're there, maybe you can help me."

Cheryl dove into her pussy headfirst, slurping, sucking, and licking away, causing Diana's body to shake. It felt so good that she felt waves of electricity shoot from her head to her toes.

"Yesss, right there. That feels so good. Don't stop!" Diana moaned while she continued slurping away between her legs. Her eyes were closed and her hands caressed the back of her head. She ate her pussy like it was sirloin steak, not ignoring one spot. "Oh my God. I'm so fucking horny right now."

Diana had been with a few guys, but never had she experienced this kind of pleasure before. Especially from a woman. She had heard stories about how good they were in bed, but now to her satisfaction, she was getting a first-hand lesson. It was the best oral sex of her life. If her tongue could do this to her body, she couldn't wait to see what kind of performance her fingers would do.

"Oh my goodness, stick your fingers in," Diana blurted out, trying to push Cheryl's head away from her vagina. She kept a firm grip on her legs so she couldn't escape.

"Chill out, I know what I'm doing," Cheryl said, standing up.

She took off her nightgown, standing there in just her panties, no bra, and started fondling her titties. Diana watched her partner perform right in front of her. After she sucked her own breasts, the two of them got into the sixty-nine position and sucked each other's pussies until they both came. They went back to Cheryl's bedroom and continued their sexual acts until they both fell asleep.

TWENTY-ONE

With the prison still on lockdown, everyone was starting to get antsy. There was nothing to do, and the only movement you had was from your bunk to the dayroom or the bathroom. The superintendent ordered a bunch of PlayStation 4s for all the blocks, trying to keep the peace within the institution. Monroe and his coworkers were still housed over in the infirmary, and then you still had a couple of workers that had been pulled to work on the K block units. Other than that, there was hardly anything going on.

Anna came in for her shift and walked past Monroe like she didn't see him. Usually she would speak to all the workers, but she didn't speak to anyone. She went into the nurses' station briefly, then headed to the break room. Monroe wanted to see if she was okay, so he walked toward the back and stood by the linen closet. He even locked the door so she could open it when she came out.

"Excuse me, Ms. A, can you open this door for me?" he asked when she exited the break room. At first she was about to walk by like she didn't hear him, but stopped and pulled out her keys. "Did I do something to you?"

"What you think? What is this I'm hearing that Paula seen your dick?" She stood there while he stood inside the room.

"What are you talking about? She hasn't seen anything," he denied. "When did this supposedly happened?"

"The other night when I couldn't make it down here. She was talking to us in the break room about seeing one of the worker's dicks, saying that it was humongous. The first person I thought about was you because she damn sure wasn't talking about any of the other workers."

"How do you know it was me? Why couldn't it have been one of them she was talking about?"

"Don't play with me, Monroe. I know it wasn't them because they're white. Besides, she said it was huge and black. You're black. Do the math."

Monroe thought about it for a moment, realizing that she had a valid point. Hopefully the only thing she said was she saw it. It took him a few seconds to respond.

"The only way she saw my dick was if she saw me pissing. Other than that, she didn't see shit, and stop letting people get to you like that. I'm assuming nobody knows about us, so she can't be saying it to rub you the wrong way. That has to be it. She saw me using the bathroom. Matter of fact, she did walk through the bathroom when I was in there. She was passing by going to the other room."

"That better be all she seen," Anna said, calming down. "I'm sorry if I seemed mad. I just don't want to share you unless I get to pick the other person."

That fucked Monroe up. Did she just say what he thought she said? So she was willing to have a threesome, but only if she got to pick the third party? He had to try his luck.

"So if I wanted to have a threesome, who

would you pick? I'm just curious." Monroe smiled, hoping she didn't get mad.

"It wouldn't be none of these bitches here, that's for sure," she replied. She looked around to make sure no one was looking, then stepped inside the threshold of the closet. She stuck her hand down the sweatpants he was wearing and rubbed his dick. "I'm not sharing this with none of these thirsty bitches."

"But if you had to, which one would you choose?"

He was really trying to get her to pick one so then he could try to persuade her to have it. He just hoped she didn't say one of the ugly nurses to be smart. You know how when females feel threatened by another female, they will not want them involved because they think you will want to keep seeing that person and leave you alone.

"I would probably pick either Kayley or Sara. They seem like they would be down for it. The rest of them probably would try and snitch on us because they hate the fact that I'm the most wanted in this place."

Monroe placed his hand on her pussy and slid a finger across the slit. Then he squeezed her breast through her shirt. She loved the way he touched her body. It made her feel like she was twenty-one again.

"Why don't you test the waters and see if they would be down?" Anna stopped, pulled her hand from his pants, and stared at him. "Never mind, I don't want you to get mad."

"I have to go, but meet me in Iso 1 in five minutes. If you make me cum better than you ever have, I'll consider doing that for you. But it has to be a powerful one for me to even attempt to ask them to do something like that."

"I got you, trust me!" Monroe replied, stepping out of the closet. He couldn't wait until she came back. The good thing was, she didn't know about Paula.

~ ~ ~

Karen was just getting home from a doctor's appointment when she saw Taylor coming out of the house with her daughter. She stepped out of the car and walked toward them.

"Hey, Trinity. What's up, Taylor?" They both waved to her. "You have a minute to talk?"

"Trinity, go get in the car, I'll be right there." As soon as Trinity sat in the car, she turned to Karen. "What's up?"

"Ashley said that you didn't want to be in the club anymore."

"I enjoyed that night a little too much, but I'm not gay. I can't be doing that," Taylor said in an apologetic manner. She really had been thinking about that night, and as much as her pussy would moisten up when she did, she knew it wasn't right. She had to be a good role model for her daughter. "You can understand where I'm coming from, right?"

"I do, but you joined us because your good-for-nothing husband is never around. I killed someone because they were trying to hurt you, Taylor. If that gets out, we all go down, if you know what I mean." She said it as more of a threat than anything else, and Taylor knew it.

"Are you threatening me?"

"Now why would I do that?" Karen said, then headed in the house without explaining herself.

Taylor got in the car with her daughter and pulled off. At that moment, she knew it was the calm before the storm.

~ ~ ~

"Take it out, Monroe! Take it out, it hurts!"

"Relax your muscles and stop tightening up. You'll like it."

"No, it hurts. Put it back in my pussy, baby, come on."

He pulled his dick out of her ass and slid right back into her pussy, pumping away. He was hitting her with vicious strokes, as if he was trying to break her back. They were going at it so hard that they kept changing positions from doggy style to her riding him while he sat in a chair that he brought in.

Monroe squeezed her plump, round ass and stared at her flat stomach and small waist as she rode up and down on his dick. Her perky breasts bounced and jiggled wildly as she caressed her dark brown nipples while biting her full bottom lip. Her pussy was so wet and extremely warm that her juices felt like soothing warm water running down his abdominal area as it secreted to his balls and thighs.

"Fuck me. Fuck me harder, baby!" she moaned. They were sitting in the back area of Iso 1 near the tub as she rode Monroe backward. "That's it, daddy, that's my spot right there. This dick is so good! Tear this pussy up."

"This how you want it, huh?"

She felt herself about to cum and turned around so she was now facing him. Monroe watched her eyes roll to the back of her head as she dug her fingernails in his chest.

"Don't stop, I'm about to cum. Oh shiiiittt, I'm cumming!"

Her body began to quake and quiver as she let out a deep invigorating sigh which caused Monroe to tense up also. Before they knew it, they were both exploding together. After he released his semen inside her, he got up and used a towel to wipe himself.

"Let me see that towel," Anna said, breathing heavily. She had one pants leg hanging off her leg. Monroe passed her the towel. "Thank you!"

Once she wiped the semen from her pussy, they quickly got dressed and walked out of the room. As soon as they came through the double doors, Sergeant Reed was walking from K block. He stopped and looked at both of them mysteriously. Neither said anything.

"What were you two doing?"

To Be Continued

Forbidden Pleasure Part 2
"Never Say Never"
Coming Soon!

To order books, please fill out the order form below:
To order films please go to www.good2gofilms.com

Name:_____

Address:_____

City:_____State:_____Zip Code: _____

Phone:_____

Email:_____

Method of Payment: Check   VISA MASTERCARD

Credit Card#:_ _____

Name as it appears on card: _____

Signature: _____

Item Name	Price	Qty	Amount
48 Hours to Die – Silk White	$14.99		
A Hustler's Dream – Ernest Morris	$14.99		
A Hustler's Dream 2 – Ernest Morris	$14.99		
A Thug's Devotion – J. L. Rose and J. M. McMillon	$14.99		
All Eyes on Tommy Gunz – Warren Holloway	$14.99		
Black Reign – Ernest Morris	$14.99		
Bloody Mayhem Down South – Trayvon Jackson	$14.99		
Bloody Mayhem Down South 2 – Trayvon Jackson	$14.99		
Business Is Business – Silk White	$14.99		
Business Is Business 2 – Silk White	$14.99		
Business Is Business 3 – Silk White	$14.99		
Cash In Cash Out – Assa Raymond Baker	$14.99		
Cash In Cash Out 2 – Assa Raymond Baker	$14.99		
Childhood Sweethearts – Jacob Spears	$14.99		
Childhood Sweethearts 2 – Jacob Spears	$14.99		
Childhood Sweethearts 3 – Jacob Spears	$14.99		
Childhood Sweethearts 4 – Jacob Spears	$14.99		
Connected To The Plug – Dwan Marquis Williams	$14.99		
Connected To The Plug 2 – Dwan Marquis Williams	$14.99		
Connected To The Plug 3 – Dwan Williams	$14.99		
Cost of Betrayal – W.C. Holloway	$14.99		
Cost of Betrayal 2 – W.C. Holloway	$14.99		
Deadly Reunion – Ernest Morris	$14.99		
Dream's Life – Assa Raymond Baker	$14.99		
Flipping Numbers – Ernest Morris	$14.99		
Flipping Numbers 2 – Ernest Morris	$14.99		

Forbidden Pleasure – Ernest Morris	$14.99		
He Loves Me, He Loves You Not – Mychea	$14.99		
He Loves Me, He Loves You Not 2 – Mychea	$14.99		
He Loves Me, He Loves You Not 3 – Mychea	$14.99		
He Loves Me, He Loves You Not 4 – Mychea	$14.99		
He Loves Me, He Loves You Not 5 – Mychea	$14.99		
Killing Signs – Ernest Morris	$14.99		
Killing Signs 2 – Ernest Morris	$14.99		
Kings of the Block – Dwan Willams	$14.99		
Kings of the Block 2 – Dwan Willams	$14.99		
Lord of My Land – Jay Morrison	$14.99		
Lost and Turned Out – Ernest Morris	$14.99		
Love & Dedication – W.C. Holloway	$14.99		
Love Hates Violence – De'Wayne Maris	$14.99		
Love Hates Violence 2 – De'Wayne Maris	$14.99		
Love Hates Violence 3 – De'Wayne Maris	$14.99		
Love Hates Violence 4 – De'Wayne Maris	$14.99		
Married To Da Streets – Silk White	$14.99		
M.E.R.C. – Make Every Rep Count Health and Fitness	$14.99		
Mercenary In Love – J.L. Rose & J.L. Turner	$14.99		
Money Make Me Cum – Ernest Morris	$14.99		
My Besties – Asia Hill	$14.99		
My Besties 2 – Asia Hill	$14.99		
My Besties 3 – Asia Hill	$14.99		
My Besties 4 – Asia Hill	$14.99		
My Boyfriend's Wife – Mychea	$14.99		
My Boyfriend's Wife 2 – Mychea	$14.99		
My Brothers Envy – J. L. Rose	$14.99		
My Brothers Envy 2 – J. L. Rose	$14.99		
Naughty Housewives – Ernest Morris	$14.99		
Naughty Housewives 2 – Ernest Morris	$14.99		
Naughty Housewives 3 – Ernest Morris	$14.99		
Naughty Housewives 4 – Ernest Morris	$14.99		
Never Be The Same – Silk White	$14.99		
Scarred Faces – Assa Raymond Baker	$14.99		

Scarred Knuckles – Assa Raymond Baker	$14.99		
Shades of Revenge – Assa Raymond Baker	$14.99		
Slumped – Jason Brent	$14.99		
Someone's Gonna Get It – Mychea	$14.99		
Stranded – Silk White	$14.99		
Supreme & Justice – Ernest Morris	$14.99		
Supreme & Justice 2 – Ernest Morris	$14.99		
Supreme & Justice 3 – Ernest Morris	$14.99		
Tears of a Hustler – Silk White	$14.99		
Tears of a Hustler 2 – Silk White	$14.99		
Tears of a Hustler 3 – Silk White	$14.99		
Tears of a Hustler 4 – Silk White	$14.99		
Tears of a Hustler 5 – Silk White	$14.99		
Tears of a Hustler 6 – Silk White	$14.99		
The Last Love Letter – Warren Holloway	$14.99		
The Last Love Letter 2 – Warren Holloway	$14.99		
The Panty Ripper – Reality Way	$14.99		
The Panty Ripper 3 – Reality Way	$14.99		
The Solution – Jay Morrison	$14.99		
The Teflon Queen – Silk White	$14.99		
The Teflon Queen 2 – Silk White	$14.99		
The Teflon Queen 3 – Silk White	$14.99		
The Teflon Queen 4 – Silk White	$14.99		
The Teflon Queen 5 – Silk White	$14.99		
The Teflon Queen 6 – Silk White	$14.99		
The Vacation – Silk White	$14.99		
Tied To A Boss – J.L. Rose	$14.99		
Tied To A Boss 2 – J.L. Rose	$14.99		
Tied To A Boss 3 – J.L. Rose	$14.99		
Tied To A Boss 4 – J.L. Rose	$14.99		
Tied To A Boss 5 – J.L. Rose	$14.99		
Time Is Money – Silk White	$14.99		
Tomorrow's Not Promised – Robert Torres	$14.99		
Tomorrow's Not Promised 2 – Robert Torres	$14.99		
Two Mask One Heart – Jacob Spears and Trayvon Jackson	$14.99		
Two Mask One Heart 2 – Jacob Spears and Trayvon Jackson	$14.99		

Two Mask One Heart 3 – Jacob Spears and Trayvon Jackson	$14.99		
Wrong Place Wrong Time – Silk White	$14.99		
Young Goonz – Reality Way	$14.99		
Subtotal:			
Tax:			
Shipping (Free) U.S. Media Mail:			
Total:			

Make Checks Payable To: Good2Go Publishing, 7311 W Glass Lane, Laveen, AZ 85339

CPSIA information can be obtained
at www.ICGtesting.com
Printed in the USA
LVHW021930030921
696898LV00012B/337

9 781947 340565